BLOOD HOLIDAY

BLOOD HOLIDAY

THE DIVINE VAMPIRE HEIRS, BOOK 2.5

A Holiday Novella

by

GINNA MORAN

For Amy Holliday and her love of vampires.

THE DAYS OF THE DIVIDE

"PLEASE, DON'T MAKE ME." I drop the metallic-lettered invitation onto the table in front of me. "Can't we just do something here?"

Diego plops down in the seat next to me, shifting my legs across his lap. Gathering my hands between his, he pulls them to his mouth and kisses the backs of each of them. "I won't, but Mitchell will. It's tradition, and one of the few holidays we celebrate."

"Some holiday," I murmur without looking at Diego. I know if I do, I'll lose myself in the stormy depths of his intense gaze.

His cool lips brush over my wrists. "The worst. I don't exactly like celebrating the Days of The Divide, either, but it's also the start of Winter Nights."

"Which is the time of year I used to fear most." I hate that I just admitted that, but it's true. No human in their right mind would celebrate such an occasion. Nights already felt too long in The Boxes, even in the summer. But now? I should be grateful. It means my guys get to have more time out of the confines of the Divinity Estate. We can have longer date nights. I just can't shake the ingrained fear that always came with winter.

"I hope to change that, beautiful," he whispers, tugging me closer until I shift off my chair and onto him. He adjusts my legs so that I straddle his lap to face him, not allowing me to keep my attention on the invitation.

I smile and peek up at him, unable to resist his need for my affection. "You already have. But can't the four of us celebrate? Why travel? Why personally invite me? Who is that guy even?"

"That guy is a board member, and you're a Divine Heir."

"A *future* Divine Heir. I'm not one yet."

"Yet."

He's right about that. Because I promised my guys forever. For once in my life, I got to make a decision for my future that was solely for me. I nearly can't believe that it'll happen. If only it wasn't so hard carrying the reminder of what I'm sacrificing for eternity.

Suppressing thoughts of my sister, I purse my lips and hold Diego's gaze. "I can't wait, you know."

"Me either." Diego grins and fiddles with the chain on my neck, trailing his fingers torturously slow down my cleavage to mess with the vow pendant.

I cover his hand with my own, rubbing my finger across the heavy ring on his finger with a drop of my blood, a reminder of my own promise to him. "Yeah?" I only say it because I love hearing the words.

Releasing the necklace, he draws his hand to my shoulder to push back my hair. "More than you know. Which is why I know that everything will be fine with the holidays. I promise. It's a small gathering of vampires and nothing extravagant. Might be more fun than you think."

"Or awkward."

He chuckles. "Never. We'll get through it, even if we have to sneak away. I've been dying to take you outside the Divinity Estate more. It might get your mind off—"

I touch my fingers to his lips so that he doesn't say my sister's name out loud. "I expect lots of distractions and all the sneaking." I graze my lips to his, sinking into him while wrapping my arms around his neck.

Diego reacts to my kiss by tightening his hold and standing up. Gliding his tongue into my mouth, he sets off a wave of desire inside me I'll use to block out the rest of the world. I've been waiting all night for him to make a move that surpasses the sweet kisses he showers me with.

His hands slide up my dress to squeeze the smooth skin of my ass peeking out from the lacy underwear in his favorite blue color. "Is this okay?"

"Better than okay."

He hums in his throat. "I've been waiting to do this all night."

We only make it a few feet toward the bed before a tap sounds on the door. I pull away and glance at the door, hearing the soft voices of Austin and Kingston in the hallway outside. Diego groans and sets me on my feet, knowing his brothers well enough to know that they won't leave us alone until I respond. He also knows me well enough to know that I'd never send them away, especially before dinner.

But just because they're outside doesn't mean I can't give Diego another minute more. Wiggling my fingers, I motion for him to close the space. I kiss him again despite the tap growing louder. He devours my attention, smiling his brilliant smile through kisses.

And then the banging begins.

"Babe, are you seriously going to ignore us?" Kingston

asks through the door.

"No, but I am," Diego says. "You can wait. Our girl needs another moment."

Diego attempts to lift me off my feet, and I giggle and wag my finger at him.

"It's just for a few minutes," I say, biting my lip between my teeth.

"I expect more than that," Kingston mutters. "It's already been hours."

"Don't listen to him. We can come back when you're ready, Jewel," Austin says.

I turn my gaze to Diego, and he shrugs. "No, it's okay. I've missed you both. Come on in."

The door flies open a second later, and Diego scoops me off my feet, making me shriek. I expect him to play keep away with his brothers, but he surprises me by tossing me in their direction. My head spins, and I screech again. All three of them laugh, amused as hell by my reaction. Austin catches me and turns his back toward Kingston, stopping him from snatching me away. I smack my hands on Austin's chest, heaving a breath. If I didn't love how cute they are when they mess with me like this, they'd be in all sorts of trouble.

I bury my face in the crook of Austin's neck and press my lips to his skin. "A little warning next time."

"What's the fun in that?" he asks, shifting me away from

Kingston again.

"If you didn't always make those sexy ass noises, maybe we'd stop." Kingston sucks in his bottom lip. "You have to pull yourself together, babe."

"It's good for your reflexes, too," Diego says.

"Like I'm going to believe that's the only reason."

Kingston chuckles. "It's not even close to number one of the reasons why."

I roll my eyes at him and inhale another breath. Austin kisses my forehead without a word, but he doesn't have to say anything for me to know he agrees with Kingston.

Tilting my face up, I kiss Austin sweetly, just brushing my lips lightly over his. He tightens his hold on me, trailing his hands lower down my body. "If you want some extra affection, all you have to do is ask."

"Babe, I need all the extra affection. Come here. It's been forever," Kingston says from behind me.

I laugh against Austin's lips because he doesn't release me. His hand shifts away, and from the growl Kingston releases, he very well could have flipped him off. He's sneaky like that. Last week I caught him doing so in the mirror but chose not to say anything. Kingston definitely deserves it most of the time.

"It's been hours," I murmur, pulling back slightly.

"Same difference."

Austin relents to my wiggling and sets me on my feet, his vibrant green eyes smiling at me brighter than the cute smirk plastered across his lips. I pat his cheek and turn to Kingston, who stands with his arms crossed over his chest. His tousled hair hangs over his forehead, hiding his midnight eyes, darker than the night outside the tinted glass window.

"You sure?" I ask him. "Because...look at this space. I don't think you've missed me that much."

One second I'm next to Austin, and in the next, my back rests against the cool window as I perch on the high window seat. Kingston stands between my legs and leans into me, resting his forehead to mine without kissing me.

"Is this close enough for you?" he asks, only brushing his pouty lips to mine with his words.

"Not quite." I caress my lips to his, feeling the soft hum of his murmur vibrating over my skin.

"Any closer and I'll need to take you back to our room."

"I guess this will have to do."

He groans and kisses me deeper. "All right, Austin. I wanna switch days. I'll do anything."

"Not a chance," Austin says, smiling at me from over Kingston's shoulder.

"Oh, come on," Kingston complains.

I touch Kingston's cheeks to stop him from turning

away from me to glare at his brother. "Don't even. Austin and I already made plans."

"That will have to change." Diego swipes the stupid holiday invitation from the table. I had nearly forgotten about the thing with my guys giving me all their attention. "This was delivered earlier."

Kingston disappears from between my legs to stand next to Diego. Austin joins them next, and I scoot off the window seat and watch their faces, hoping for a reaction. None of them give me anything.

"This should be interesting," Kingston says, glancing at me. He doesn't say what's on his mind, but from his puckering brow, I can tell something bothers him. He won't tell me what, though. I'll have to rely on Austin to give into my need for answers. Kingston would rather keep me in the dark despite how annoyed it makes me.

"It's going to be fine," Diego reminds me.

I raise an eyebrow. "Are you sure about that?"

Diego elbows Kingston. "Tell her."

Kingston sighs, throwing his hands up. "It's going to be fine...and interesting."

"Or awful," I mutter under my breath.

"That too."

It's Austin's turn to elbow him. "Knock it off. We're all going to have fun. Don't freak her out for nothing. She's going to love it."

"You think so?" I ask.

Austin smiles at me. "It's a good time to start immersing you in our social circles. Plus, we can start new traditions together. Maybe do something familiar your family used to do."

I scrunch my nose. "I never celebrated any holiday outside of a birthday, and even then, it felt like a regular day. Mom would cook our favorite meal."

"What? No other holidays? I thought some humans kept up ones from the back-world," Kingston says. "Actually, I know they have. I can't believe you've never celebrated anything."

Lifting and dropping my shoulders, I say, "What was there for me to celebrate? For my last birthday, I waited in line for my first gen. pop. blood donation. Not exactly a party."

All three of them fall silent, thinking over my words. Their obvious pouty expressions reveal how much my words bother them and how much they want things to be different. But it's whatever to me. I couldn't care less about turning one day out of the year into something special. I'd like all of them to be. And they are.

"I'm sorry, Jewel," Austin finally says.

"It's fine. Wasn't important."

Sliding his hand around my back, Austin pulls me to him. "But I'd like it to be."

"We can try, I guess." His eyes light up at my words and willingness to give this whole holiday thing a shot. For my guys, I'll do anything. Even join them to celebrate something that'll have my dad cursing from death. "How do you all even celebrate The Divide anyway?"

Kingston tosses the invitation in the trash. "Reenactments."

I blanch, my cheeks cooling at his words. That sounds awful. Everything I know about the divisions makes my stomach churn. Donor Life Corp separated families. They divided cities and corralled humans. It's something I can't ever imagine happening now. My grandparents and great-grandparents barely survived.

Austin punches Kingston so hard in the ribs that he stumbles sideways. "He's mostly kidding, Jewel. We personally don't reenact anything. We only exchange gifts and party. Kind of like a back-world holiday, if you know anything about them."

Hugging myself, I study all three of their faces, knowing that Kingston wasn't really kidding and there is truth to his words. But they want to keep it from me. How could I blame them for wanting to protect me? I straighten my shoulders. "So it's mostly like a Christmas movie? I've seen one of those."

Diego nods. "Without the guy in a red suit."

Kingston frowns, clearly torn by what he revealed. "I think you forgot about the man last year. Don't you remember how much blood was on him? It was basically like he was wearing a—"

One wide-eyed look from me shuts Kingston up, and the three of them surround me in the most comforting group hug I could ask for. I mean, damn. My body feels like it's going to split so a part of me can follow each of them as they back a foot away.

I puff out my bottom lip. "Are you sure we can't skip?"

"Sorry, babe," Kingston says. "It's mandatory. A way to keep the peace. But you know what? Austin was right, and you know how much I hate admitting that. It'll be fun."

"Fun? Yeah, right."

"We'll make it so for you, Jewel," Austin says.

"Maybe add a little back-world holiday cheer," Diego adds.

I inhale a long breath. "With lights and presents?"

"Possibly snow."

"Snow?" I've never seen snow. The thought of seeing such a sight brings an automatic smile to my face.

Diego nods. "And we'll watch all the holiday classics your heart can handle."

Kingston smirks at me, relaxing a bit now that I have. "You forgot kissing under the mistletoe. I'll assure lots of that."

"What, no biting?" I ask. "That seems like something you all would enjoy."

Diego tips his head back and laughs.

Kingston snaps his teeth at me. "I guess we'll find out."

"I can't wait," I tease. And it's true. I never thought celebrating a vampire holiday would be something I'd want to experience, but with the excitement now radiating between us, I think it's exactly what I need.

This is going to be my forever after all.

"And we're definitely not going to make you, babe." He turns to Austin. "Find the damn mistletoe now."

"Now?"

He chuckles. "I'm feeling rather starved."

BLOODY INTERRUPTIONS

"ARE YOU SHITTING ME? IT lasts a few days, and we have to travel together with Mitchell?" I ask, staring at the glowing dashboard. "I'll never survive."

It's one thing to have to deal with the occasional drop-in from my guys' dad, but it's another to have to share the same breathing space with him for an extended period of time, especially after he broke into my mind and allowed Donor Life Corp to give Ramona to Orlando to fulfill my family's blood debt.

Sure, we still have time to figure out how to get her out of it without putting me in her place before she turns eighteen, but it still weighs heavy on me. Shit happens. It has happened. It's only been three weeks since she was taken, but it's felt like eternity.

And my feelings over that effed up situation can't even compare to how I feel about what Orlando did to Brayla...

I push the thought away. If I think about her for another second, I'll break down and cry. The last thing I want is for Mitchell to catch me crying. He doesn't understand the turmoil that hides inside me, brought on by his vulgar ways. Or how much I never want to seem weak in front of him. He likes it too much. He'll use it against us like he used me against Diego, Austin, and Kingston to get his way with the Blood Rebels.

Austin senses me shutting down with my racing memories and pulls me into a hug. He kisses me to distract me in the best way possible. "I know it isn't ideal—"

I lean back an inch, managing to keep my shit together. "You think? I thought we'd meet him there. This sucks."

Kingston grabs onto my legs and slings them over his lap, scooting even closer so that I'm sandwiched between him and Austin. He tightens his jaw. "It's a short drive and better to travel together. We'll be leaving the Divine Region for our stay on Mount Crescent. It's neutral territory split between board members. They're already there and waiting."

I groan. "The board members?"

He nods. "At least it's not all of them."

Diego looks at me in the rearview mirror. "And they'll be plenty occupied strategizing against each other."

"We'll be busy doing our own thing as well," Austin adds. He rests his chin on my shoulder. "Promise."

The front passenger's side door slams, startling me, and Mitchell swivels in his seat, beaming me his charming smile. "He's right about that, Jewel. You'll be plenty entertained." He looks to each of his sons. "I'm glad you could all join me for the trip."

Like we even had a choice.

"We wouldn't miss it," Kingston says, rubbing his hands up and down my legs to keep the chill away. I regret not wearing pants, but I wanted to look nice in case. My guys all wear suits. So does Mitchell.

Diego puts the car in drive, and we take off, leaving the Divinity Estate in a wake of smoke from his sudden stomping of the throttle. Austin adjusts the seatbelt restraints around me, and I rest my head on his shoulder, ignoring the fact that I can feel Mitchell's eyes glued to me.

No one says anything as Diego drives us away from the safety of our home. I do my best to distract myself by sliding my fingers in and out of Austin's over and over again, but nothing works. This car ride is miserable.

"If you're going to keep squirming like that, you should

just sit on my lap," Kingston quips, drawing my attention to him.

"Kingston." My cheeks burn at his comment. "Seriously? In front of Mitchell?"

"And in front of us," Diego says.

He chuckles. "Just thinking about keeping Jewel busy."

"I think I'll just sleep," I say, moving my leg to caress my hand over his lap. "Wake me up when we get there."

"Tease," he whispers, leaning his head back.

Silence draws between the five of us. If it were just my guys and me, it'd be different. But we've all been kind of on edge around Mitchell lately. With good reason. Fucker.

"Boys," Mitchell finally says after another quiet few minutes. He annoyingly keeps his voice at a pitch I shouldn't be able to hear. "I expect you three to be on your best behavior this trip. Do not discuss any Divine matters and keep Jewel out of the way the best you can. I don't like her wild dramatics when it comes to donor affairs. You must teach her better control."

I keep my eyes closed as to not react to his words. He sounds like it's a burden that I'm joining them, but he also probably knew that my guys would never leave me behind.

"We're working on it," Diego says in a whisper. "You'll be pleasantly surprised by her adjustment."

It's a flat out lie, but now I'm going to have to work extra hard to stay expressionless to make sure not to prove Diego wrong.

"And we'll keep her plenty busy," Kingston whispers, sneaking his hand under the hem of my dress.

Shutting my legs, I trap his fingers in place before he gets carried away. I peek at his wide ass smile through my lashes, seeing how much he enjoys teasing me. He flashes his fangs at me, and I stick out my tongue. Austin loosens the restraints to let me get comfortable. I silently shimmy down and rest my head on Austin's lap, making Kingston sigh because I don't continue to joke around, but I can still feel Mitchell's attention burning into me even if he doesn't look.

Austin plays with my hair, ignoring Mitchell. "You hungry?" he asks me to fill the silence. He can tell that there's no way I'll actually be able to fall asleep.

I shake my head. "Bored. Can't get comfortable, and you guys are quiet as hell." I purposely add the last part to continue my act. I'm so glad I can hear their whispering. It must be unsettling for the humans who hang around vampires and can't. I'd go crazy from the silence.

"It's only for—"

The car thuds over something, and I jostle in my seat, bouncing at the sudden change in terrain. Kingston and Austin hold me tighter, keeping me in place. I struggle to sit up, fear clenching my chest. I can't help it. The last time something like this happened to the car, we were attacked by Blood Rebels.

Diego swears, gripping the wheel in an attempt to regain control. "Damn it. Flat tire."

"What'd you hit?" Kingston asks, bracing one hand to the front seat.

"Don't know. I didn't see anything."

After Diego jabs a few buttons on the dash, the car finally smooths out. I clutch onto Austin's hand and sit up to peer out the windshield. Diego looks at me in the rearview mirror with a frown.

"Diego, swerve!" Mitchell grabs the wheel and the world spins, sending me ramming into Kingston.

I screech from the movement and squeeze my eyes shut. Once again, the world bounces around until we come to a complete stop. Dirt clouds the air in front of us, and I gulp in a few breaths. Austin rushes to unbuckle me from my seat, running his hands along my body in the process to check me out the best he can without taking a peek under my dress.

"Are you hurt?" he asks just to make sure.

"I—I don't think—" Two hands smack the window, cutting off my words. I scream.

Kingston, Diego, and Mitchell abandon the car, slamming their doors. Austin activates the locks and grabs my face in his hands in an attempt to stop me from looking out the dark window. He inspects every inch of my face, though I can tell his mind wanders to what's happening outside.

"I need you to try to stay calm," Austin says, keeping his voice low.

I bob my head. "Got it."

A body hits the window, and I startle and release an uncontrollable, breathless sob.

"Shit balls! I don't got it. What the hell is going on?" My words tumble from my mouth faster than my heart races in an attempt to escape my chest. It wants nothing more than to splatter on Austin's lap so that he can take better care of it than my body can.

"Not sure. Think it might have been a trap set by some city dwellers. The roads outside our region aren't monitored as closely," he says, rubbing his hands up and down my arms.

"A trap? Are the shadow vampires insane? Don't they realize—"

Austin kisses the scream from me as an unfamiliar face collides into the window. I pull away from him to gawk at the vampire. He snaps his teeth at me, his silver eyes glowing unlike anything I've seen. He freaks me the eff out with the way his eyes narrow on me like he can see the blood pumping through my veins. Snarling, he pounds his fists to the glass, trying to break through the barrier between us.

"Look away from him," Austin says.

"What's wrong with him?"

"By the looks of this desolate area, he's probably starving. The mark on his forehead means he's been banned from whatever city he might have once called home."

"Banned? You guys do that?" I ask. I never heard of such a thing.

He nods his head, darting his eyes to look out the window again. "If it isn't a terrible offense. Sometimes, it's temporary. Better than a death sentence. Every region is different."

I follow his gaze and study the five weird fading lines tattooed into the vampire's forehead. "I guess you have to maintain order somehow, huh? Not just with humans."

Austin doesn't get a chance to respond. Blood sprays over the window as a blade cuts right through the man's eye from the back of his head. I don't even have time to react before Austin shields me from the grotesque view and swears under his breath. If his lips weren't pressed to my ear, I would've missed it.

Silence falls over the car apart from the rapping of my heart, and Austin embraces me for a long moment, stroking his fingers up and down the length of my back. A knock on the window stiffens my muscles until I hear Kingston and Diego murmuring to each other.

"It's over, Jewel. It's okay. We're all fine," Austin says, letting me go.

"You just might not want to look outside the car, beautiful," Diego says through the glass. The door opens, letting in cool air, and I shiver.

"Unless you want to throw up." Kingston leans in and blocks my view, knowing me well enough that I can't help myself and will look regardless of their suggestion. "Which none of us wants."

"Hurry up and get in, sons." Mitchell gets behind the wheel before Diego. "We don't have all night. This little interruption put us behind schedule."

Kingston motions for Austin to scoot over, and Austin picks me up and slides to the middle at the same time, holding me on his lap. Kingston bumps him with his shoulder, flaring his nostrils, but he won't say anything because it's Austin's night.

Diego gets into the front next to Mitchell and offers me his brilliant smile. Twisting, he reaches back and links his hand through mine, swinging our arms for a moment. With the way everyone's acting, it's like they didn't even fight some outcast vampires or stab one through the eye. I still sometimes can't shake how normal it is to them to annihilate the enemy. But I should be used to it. I've done it myself with Katherine Duchanne, the bitch who tried to steal me from my guys to get revenge.

Mitchell messes with the dashboard, and the headlights illuminate the land in front of us to show a couple of bloody forms in the dirt. The car jolts forward, bouncing me in the seat again as Mitchell runs over them. And then the car dies. The lights blink off, leaving us in darkness. Austin shifts me to sit on the seat between him and Kingston, and the two of them lean forward for a better look of what's going on.

"We can either wait here for a staff member to bring us a new vehicle or finish the trek by foot," Mitchell says.

I expect my guys to tell him that we'll wait, but they all throw their doors open.

"Wait, we're walking?" I ask.

"It's not far, beautiful," Diego says. "We can call for another car when we get there."

"Better to keep moving, my dear." Mitchell peers around. "You never know who might be hiding in wait for a taste of my magnificent future heir."

I grimace at his words, though I know they're intended to be a compliment.

"Yeah, babe. If you think you're a savage, you have no ide—"

Austin shoves Kingston out of the car, and he quickly hops to his feet and flashes his fangs.

"Quit it. She doesn't have to worry about any of that,"

Austin says.

"He's right, beautiful. Kingston's just being an asshole because he loves how clingy you get when you're scared."

Kingston wags his eyebrows at me. "There are ten other ways I can get Jewel to cling to me—"

"Dude, Kingston, seriously," I say.

He has the nerve to wink.

I sigh and let Austin help me to my feet and out of the car. He twines our fingers together, keeping me close to his side. We watch Diego pop the trunk to get our bags, and Kingston holds up a backpack to me with Austin's medical supplies. I adjust it onto my shoulders without waiting for him to help, and then Austin swivels and bends lower, motioning for me to jump on his back.

"I need you to hold on tight, okay?" he says when I hook my legs and arms around him.

I rest my head on his shoulder. "Should I be worried?"

"Not a chance, beautiful. Just take a breath and relax," Diego says, sliding his hand between my back and the bag to rub smooth circles over me for a moment.

I inhale a small breath and snuggle Austin close. "I'll try my best."

"Everyone set?" Mitchell asks, adjusting his bag on his shoulder. It's so strange to see him carry something for himself.

All my guys nod.

"I guess so," I murmur.

He flashes his fangs in a smile. "Then follow me."

MOUNT CRESCENT

MY BREATH FOGS IN FRONT of me. "Shit, it's cold."

Diego slips out of his suit jacket and drapes it across my shoulders. "We'll be inside in a few minutes.

"And then I'll warm you up," Kingston says, offering me his jacket to add to Diego's.

I smile as I accept it, taking a deep breath of my guys' delicious scent. Sweet and irresistible, it's a fragrance I don't mind suffocating myself in.

"Tomorrow," Austin says, rubbing his fingers back and forth on my bare legs. I'm nearly certain at this point he'll have to pry my frozen limbs from him. "Still my night."

Kingston glares. "Lucky bastard."

"And he knows it," Diego says.

Austin chuckles and manages to flip me from his back to cradle against him. I slip my icy fingers into his jacket, making him shiver, but he doesn't complain, even when I pop a button and sneak them inside his shirt. He's usually cooler than me, but with how cold the temperature keeps dropping, he feels plenty warm now.

"You feel so good," I whisper, hiding my face against his chest to breathe warm breaths in an attempt to heat up my frozen nose.

"I can say the same about you," he replies into my hair.

"Okay, that's enough. You are making me so jealous, babe." Kingston closes the space and walks backward, sandwiching me between him and Austin. Diego takes Austin's side, and it's then that I realize they're strategically surrounding me in their delicious wall of muscles and power to protect me from whatever it is they won't tell me about.

"Just make your mental list, and I'll see what I can do about it later," I tease Kingston, shifting to ruffle his hair.

He purrs in his throat. "I'm warning you now. It'll be long...and naughty."

I crack up, my laughter sounding loud enough to make me wince. My cheeks flush too. I walked right into that. "Only I can make the naughty list."

"I better be on it."

Mitchell clears his throat, drawing my attention away from Kingston's snickering, and the four of us stop behind him. Stretching my neck, I attempt to look over Kingston's shoulder, but he purposely stands taller to block my view. It takes me wiggling in Austin's arms to get him to prop me up higher for a look at the most bizarre little village I've ever seen.

"Is this for real?" I ask.

Amid the tall pine trees rest a few log cabins with red and white spiraled posts and white-painted trim along the A-line roofs. Twinkling lights twine the trees and dangle from every surface. Fake glowing animals move along the glittering pathway that leads toward a glass and wood mansion lit brightly with rainbow lights anyone could see for miles. It reminds me of the magical Christmas town from the only holiday movie among my grandpa's collection.

"Some donor traditions survived The Divide," Mitchell says, motioning toward the giant ornaments decorating the nearby trees.

"Dark Terrace Ranch never looked like this." I reach up to touch a glittering orb. It swings back and forth, sending sparkle flakes dusting over me and Austin.

Mitchell picks a red flower from a glitter-decorated potted plant and hands it to me. "Not many places do, Jewel."

I tuck the poinsettia blossom into my hair. "I wish they did. It's so pretty."

I hate admitting it, but it's true. The night has never felt so enchanting with seemingly millions of rainbow lights illuminating around us. The delectable scent of sugar wafts through the air, and soft music trickles to my ears from one of the nearby cabins.

"And it's only the start. Why don't you boys take Jewel to get settled and meet me in the main house for dinner? I'll see to it the chef prepares Jewel something festive."

Mitchell vanishes from in front of us, but I catch sight of him entering the gigantic mansion a few dozen feet ahead. Dark figures shift and move behind the tinted glass of the arched doorway. I don't stare at them for too long. My eyes just want to take in everything else.

If only the world didn't blur, sending streaks of lights across my vision.

Warm air engulfs me the second Austin stops, and I orient myself to the sudden shift in the world. Diego and Kingston bounce on their feet in the middle of a cozy living area with plush, white leather couches, a dark wood coffee table, deep blue rugs, and a glittering chandelier that sends fractals of light across the gleaming wooden floors.

Austin guides me forward and to the first room on the right. It's much smaller than the one we share at the Divinity

Estate, and it doesn't have a connected bathroom, but the bed looks inviting. If Austin wasn't holding my hand, I might make a running leap for it to dive under the downy blankets.

"This is our room," he says, waving his hand. "Not much to look at."

"Our room's over here." Diego motions me to cross the living room to the other side. Austin follows along, swinging my hand with his, and I smile at him. We look at Diego's room together, the setup mirroring Austin's, though it reminds me exactly of the room I share with Diego at home with the projector screen on the wall, the dark comforter, and an array of weapons hanging on display.

"It makes me not want to meet Mitchell later," I say, leaning on the doorframe. "I'm so cold. I just want to snuggle in bed. You're all invited to join me."

"Our room is perfect for that, babe." Kingston wiggles his fingers at me and grins, showing off his room twice as large as both Austin's and Diego's. He not only has a super king bed positioned opposite a curtained window, but he also has a massive couch wide enough to comfortably lie next to each other on.

"My brothers can take the couch," he quips, getting glowers from them.

Ignoring him, I ask, "What about Mitchell? There are

only three rooms here. Where will he stay? And if you even say in here, I'll—"

"He has a wing in the main house." Austin cuts me off before my complaint turns into a full-blown rant. "This place is solely ours."

I release a breath. "At least that's something."

Strolling away from Kingston's room, I peek my head into a friggin' awesome bathroom with the biggest tub I've ever seen. A walk-in shower gleams with glass and metal parallel from it, and I step inside the room and run my hand along one of the fluffy towels.

"Diego, why don't you start a fire, and I'll run Jewel a bath while Austin sets up his blood drawing stuff," Kingston says, rubbing his hands up and down his arms. If he's cold, then it must be freezing outside and not just my sensitive human body unable to adjust to the temperature as quickly.

"We can wait," Austin says to Kingston.

I bump my hip into Austin. "But you don't have to. I want nothing more than to feed you and get in that tub to warm up. You all look like you could use it, too."

Kingston gives me a long once-over, undressing me with his eyes. "You're the only one I'll ever share bathwater with, babe."

"That's too bad. I was going to invite you all in. It's big enough."

Kingston, Austin, and Diego all look between each other in consideration, sending heat to my cheeks. I won't need a bath to warm up with the way their intense gazes turn from each other to smolder over me.

"We did bring our swimsuits," Austin muses.

Diego chuckles at me, mapping his gaze down my body. "And Jewel looks like she really wants this."

Actually handling it might be another thing.

Kingston groans and spins around, locking his fingers through the soft locks of his hair.

"Can you all manage to behave?" I ask, trying to keep my damn smile in check. Because while we hang out all the time, this sounds like something I need to experience.

"Can you keep your hands to yourself, babe?" Kingston asks.

I laugh. "I guess you'll have to see."

"I'm down to find out." Diego takes my free hand to pull me toward the bathroom.

Austin laughs when I drag him with me. Kingston remains in his spot near his bedroom door, his dark eyes flashing silver. Diego starts the faucet to the tub, and Austin pulls his shirt over his head before tossing me the bikini I had packed instead of my usual one-pieces.

The second Kingston sees it, he heaves a sigh and crosses the room, yanking his shirt over his head. "Fuck it. I'm in."

I laugh and clap my hands. "This might be the best holiday ever."

Austin helps me unzip my dress, and I stroll toward the changing partition with my back to the three of them. Stepping out of my dress, I toss it over and Diego lets it land on his head. Austin catches my bra next, laughing with a huge ass grin on his face, his cheeks reddening.

I save my sheer underwear for last and just hang them over the side. Kingston play-growls and glares at me, striding closer. I laugh and screech, hurrying to get dressed into my bikini even though I don't care if any of them sees me naked. I just like teasing them. And they let me.

Kingston stretches over and narrows his eyes at me. "Best holiday? I think we'll see about that."

My heart refuses to slow down no matter what I try to do as I sit next to Austin in the massive spa tub. Kingston inches his way closer, begging for me to take his hand under the mountain of bubbles that stops any of us from seeing each other's bodies.

Diego holds my feet on his lap, keeping his lips pressed in a tight line every time I shift and accidentally feel his excitement. We hold each other's gaze, daring the other to react. I break first and giggle, my face flushing. My body will surely never recover from this.

"You're enjoying this way too much," Kingston says, twining my fingers through his, finally close enough to do so.

I rest our hands on his leg, making him move and softly groan. Unlike Diego, Kingston fails to hide his reaction. "Can't help it. You guys are friggin' hot."

"And you're torturing me," he quips, his jaw twitching.

I grin and release his hand to run my fingers up his rippling stomach.

"You think she's torturing you," Diego says, making me blush like crazy.

Austin chuckles and watches me in his peripheral vision, shifting as I run my other hand up and down his leg over and over again. "There's nothing torturous about any of this."

I tip my head back and laugh. "I have to agree with you."

Kingston suddenly stands up, sending a wave of bubbly water splashing over me, and Diego follows suit. Austin hooks his fingers to my side to keep me steady as we rock for a minute. I stare at the two of them grabbing towels to dry off like they didn't just abandon me.

"Okay, now I don't agree. Did I say something wrong?" I ask, attempting to stand. My hand slides across Austin's slippery shoulder, and I nearly fall under.

Kingston sighs. "Definitely not, and I wish I could get back in there with you so you can torture me more, but Mitchell's coming. No fucking way am I letting him near you in that sexy ass bikini."

Diego tugs his shirt over his damp head. "Just don't have too much fun while we're gone."

"No promises," I say, smirking at Austin.

Kingston releases an annoyed grumble and follows Diego out of the bathroom. Cool air trickles in, sending goosebumps over my skin. Austin pulls me to him, and I drape my legs over his, taking full advantage of our sudden privacy. I don't know if it's because of the change in the atmosphere or what, but he's acting more affectionate than usual, and I love it.

Diego's and Kingston's voices disappear, and I hear the sound of the front door closing.

"Is this okay?" Austin asks, trailing his hand up and down my side. "We don't have to stay in here. We can go with them. I know it's been a while since you've eaten."

"I'm good. Perfect. Exactly how I want to be right now. I'll stay in here all night if you let me. I don't care if my skin's wrinkling."

He chuckles and pulls my hand up out of the water to kiss my puckering fingers. "I'll do my best to make it happen."

I smile and lean in, brushing my lips to his. This is the first moment we've been alone in days, and I refuse to let it go to waste, especially with how sexy Austin looks right now, drinking in the sight of me every time I shift and move the bubbles away.

"That sounds like the best holiday plan ever," I whisper.

"For me, it is."

Gathering my nerves, I twist myself in Austin's lap to straddle him and kiss him in a way that sends his fingers digging into my hips. I can't help it. Adrenaline still courses through my veins from the scary encounter with the outcast shadow vampires. It helps that this whole place feels magical. I swear something different lingers in the air around this strange holiday village. Whatever it is, I want nothing more than to be with my nutrients match the way I know he desires.

Austin's muscles tighten under my touch, and he kisses me back, caressing his tongue over mine. From all my time with him, I've learned that Austin's more reserved than his brothers and will always wait for me to make the first move. I've made it my mission to be bolder with him, knowing how much he likes it.

Devouring my need to be close, Austin reacts how I had hoped, his light kiss turning desperate. Tingles blast through my whole body, and I can't stop myself from grinding against the hard bulge my closeness arouses from him.

I inhale a sharp breath at the click of his fangs extending. He grazes his teeth over my lips, careful not to break my skin, just teasing and testing me to see how I respond.

"Is this okay?" he asks, his voice deepening into a low hum that drags a whole bunch of desire from me as my body reacts in anticipation for what I hope is to come.

I moan my agreement, using my own teeth to graze over his bottom lip. I break away from him to trail my mouth along his jaw and to the damp skin of his throat. My hands work fervently down his body, exploring and memorizing every taut muscle. My fingers meet with Austin's on my hips, and I guide them up a few inches until he takes over and slides his fingers into my bikini top to graze over my breasts in a way that makes me gasp against his ear.

"Jewel." My name sounds so hot on his lips. "You're the best thing that's ever happened to me."

"I love you, Austin," I say, knowing how much he loves the admission. I straighten my back to make it easier for his mouth to kiss down my clavicle.

He nudges away my bikini top from my breast, slowly gliding his tongue lower to take it into his mouth. Bending into him, I clutch his head, running my fingers through his blond hair. My mouth chooses now to alert the world of my incredible moment with Austin, and he lifts me up with him out of the tub, kissing the embarrassing sounds away.

He sets me on the sink, pressing his hips between my legs, tangling his fingers into my hair to tug the strings of my top apart. Cool air prickles over me, and he sucks and kisses my blushing skin, hot from the tub and the raw need consuming me to take things to another level with Austin.

My fingers slip down his chest, following the line of his muscles until I reach the waistband of his swimsuit. He releases a soft moan, his back straightening. And then he slows down, bringing his hands to my face instead of where I want them to be.

Austin pulls away slightly, his chest rising and falling. "Jewel—"

"It's okay to continue," I murmur, pulling him closer.

"Jewel," he repeats in a breathless whisper, bringing his mouth back to mine for a moment. One of his fangs grazes my lip a little too hard, and his body turns rigid.

He jerks away from me, his eyes flashing silver. "I—I'm sorry. I need to stop. You're just—I'm just—I'm going to lose control if I don't."

"Oh," I say, sucking in a breath in an attempt to get my buzzing body to chill the hell out. It wants nothing more than to throw itself at Austin. But I wouldn't. Not now. Not with his brows puckering, his jaw tightening.

"I'm sorry," he repeats.

I offer him a smile. "You don't have to apologize, Austin." Tugging his hands, I pull him closer and back to me. "I understand."

And I do. Losing control is something Austin's afraid of. He's told me as much before. Even when he was severely injured by Blood Rebels in Haven Springs, he hesitated in accepting my offer to give him blood to help out. He prides himself on his restraint, and the last thing I want is to push him.

I bob my head and cup his cheeks in my hands. "And so you know, I'm not afraid of you losing control. I trust you. You're always careful with me."

He releases a long breath and smiles. "I want this. I do. But..." His words trail off as his eyes flash silver again. It's now that I realize why he struggles with himself in the moment. He never did draw my blood for dinner, and it's been longer than usual. Unlike Kingston, Austin never refrains from drinking blood. He'll still drink gen. pop. blood if he had to.

Drawing my hand from his face, I run my finger along his lips, grazing the tip over one of his fangs. He stiffens, his nostrils flaring, but he doesn't pull away.

"You're hungry," I say, tilting my head to watch the silver flash in his eyes again. "You should've told me."

He lifts and drops his shoulders. "We were having fun, and the last thing I want is for you to ever feel like a meal."

I laugh. I can't help it. "Austin, you never make me feel that way. All I ever feel is happy, because I can take care of you. You know that, right? You feed me all the time, and it's really no different."

He rubs his lips together. "I just worry sometimes."

"Is that why none of you ever ask to bite me instead of drawing my blood?" The thought has been on my mind for weeks, but it hasn't been until now, having Austin open up to me, that I get the nerve to say what I'm thinking. Because when I first Blood Matched with them, I was aware that they eventually thought we'd get to the level of me sustaining them straight from my vein.

"I can't speak for my brothers, but for me, I want it to always be pleasant for you. You're my forever, and I never want you to think you're anything less."

My heart picks up speed at his words and how considerate he is to me as more than his Blood Match. More than a future Divine Heir. And in this moment, I can envision our lives together and how perfect it'll be. Me and my three powerful vampires.

"Well, you don't have to worry about that, okay? It's been nothing short of amazing." Leaning in, I graze my lips to his. "And don't tell Kingston this, but I do find it pleasant. More than I thought I would."

Austin releases a low moan from his lips, reacting to the sudden shift in my voice. "Yeah?" he asks breathlessly.

I nod. "And if you want to now..." I let my words hang in the air and study Austin's reaction. And eff, does he give me one.

The world spins around me, his lips crashing into mine, and I suddenly find my back on the fluffiest blankets. Austin hovers over me, resting his elbow next to my ear. The look he gives me, his vibrant eyes searching desperately over me in a way that makes me feel like the most beautiful person he's ever seen, erupts a wave of warmth through me. I thought I could decipher the hunger in his eyes before, but it doesn't compare to this moment. His eyes flash, his starvation burning far deeper than needing my blood for sustenance. He looks as if only my love can truly quench the need blazing inside him that he has for me.

He combs his fingers through my wet hair, shifting it off my chest to expose my skin. I remain utterly still under him, my heart racing to out beat his. "You're stunning. Perfect."

I smile, squirming under the intensity of his gaze, all words locked in my throat.

Leaning in, he kisses me again, trailing his hands around my back to finish untying my bikini top completely to pull it away. His breath tickles my skin as his lips wander from my mouth to my jaw, and he kisses his way to my throat, taking his time to explore me with his mouth and fingers, sending my body buzzing.

I can barely handle the crazy good sensations he sets ablaze across my skin, and I release a breathless moan and slide my hands up his back to dig my fingers into his taut muscles.

"I'm ready for you to bite me," I whisper against his shoulder.

He shifts to look at me, a smile lighting his eyes. "Just a minute more."

I lean back, pulling him on top of me to feel the weight of his body against mine. Something shifts between us as I lie under him, opening myself up to be explored in a way I know he craves but wouldn't do so without my initiation. And I've never been happier to have him let his guard down for me, knowing that I'll be as careful with him as he is with me.

Austin's hands travel under me to pull my hips into his. "Will you drink from me too?"

His question stirs a thousand emotions inside me, and I'm sure if I were a vampire, my fangs would extend right about now. It's been a while since I've tasted his blood apart from his brothers, and it's never been like this. The only other times he's bitten me was in desperation during moments of injury, and doing so now in a moment of desire awakens something new between us I hadn't realized I needed in my life.

"Just a little," he adds, his gaze darting over mine as he searches for the answer I'm not quick to give.

"I'd like that," I manage to say, my voice only audible to him.

He smiles at me and bites his arm first, holding it to my lips. The subtle citrusy tang of his blood coats my tongue, sending a wave of desire through me. My whole body flushes, and I suck harder, making Austin release a moan and close his eyes. His hand slides over my breast to draw circles over the sensitive skin of my nipple, and I gasp, pulling away, and arch my back in an attempt to hide my face under the nearest pillow.

"Take a breath, Jewel," he whispers, his voice deepening in anticipation.

I do as he says, inhaling slowly, squirming under him at the gentle brush of his tongue over my chest a moment before his teeth pierce the supple skin of my breast. I cover my mouth with my hand, trying to suppress the loud ass noise that sounds like a cross between a moan and a whimper. Austin's lips take over as he sucks, his stomach rippling as he swallows.

He doesn't drink for long, just tasting me before kissing his way back to my mouth. His cool fingers put pressure on the bite mark, and he buries his face into the crook of my neck, just inhaling the scent of my hair until both of our hearts finally settle.

"Was that okay?" he asks, leaning up to meet my eyes.

I beam him a smile, biting my bottom lip between my teeth. "I forgot how friggin' amazing you taste. And now I'm starved." My stomach practically shouts its agreement.

He chuckles and tucks my hair behind my ear. "What if I tell Mitchell that you need the rest of the night to recover from the cold? As your health keeper, your condition is my top priority."

"That would be the best present ever," I say, grinning at the thought of not having to make an appearance in front of the board members here to celebrate.

"We did promise you a fun holiday," he muses, kissing me again. "I intend to assure it."

Hugging him close, I rest my head to his chest. "You already have."

Because so far, this has been the best holiday ever. And I know it's just the start.

SURPRISE

"JEWEL! FINALLY!" MY COUSINS' VOICES echo through the line as their faces appear on the screen of Kingston's phone.

Dana leans in closer, nearly pushing Fallon from view. "What have you been doing? You were supposed to call thirty minutes ago."

"Sorry, you two. I overslept," I say. "And I can't talk long. We're not at home."

"Where are you?" Fallon asks, moving her head like she can see past me through the video feed if she tries hard enough.

"The mountains. Tomorrow is the start of the celebration of the Days of The Divide for vampires." I flick my gaze to Kingston and watch him spin around and around in the rolling chair by his small desk.

He plants his feet on the floor and stops. "It's nothing special, really," he says to my cousins, though they can't see him.

My cousins look at each other. "We actually just learned about it, and no offense, but vampires are weird."

"So are humans," he says, smirking at me. "I mean, have you learned about the back-world holidays yet?"

Dana's face lights up. "Yes! Haven Springs celebrates them. It's so cool, Jewel. You would love it. Maybe you can come visit and see?"

Kingston frowns at me, and we both know that returning to Haven Springs is impossible right now. For one, I can't trust the community of exempt humans not to turn against me again, and two, it's hard enough knowing that Ramona was taken from there. To actually see my little cousins living on their own when one of us was supposed to always be there for them kills me.

"We're going to be here a while," Kingston responds, keeping his voice even. He stands behind me and peers at the screen from over my shoulder. "Maybe next year we can arrange something. Or if you tell us when the next human holiday is—"

"That would be great! We'll take pictures and send them to you," Fallon says.

A knock sounds on their door, and they both shift in their seat and look away. Dana smiles at Fallon before turning to me. "Hey, Jewel? We'll go ahead and let you go. Call us later, okay?"

"Happy holidays!" Fallon says, laughing. "That's what they say here. Merry Christmas too."

Dana bobs her head. "Happy Chanukah as well. And happy New Year. There are so many from the back-world. We get to participate in all sorts of traditions. It's so fun."

I smile at their excitement, a part of me wishing Kingston could make a trip to Haven Springs happen. "I bet. And happy holidays to you both."

The line clicks off, and I sigh, holding out Kingston's phone to him. He tosses it over his shoulder on the bed and quickly lifts me off my feet, spinning me around. I don't even get the chance to screech as his lips mold to mine, and he kisses me until I pull away and gasp in a breath.

I smile at him, so thankful he didn't even give me a moment more to think about my cousins and everything they're experiencing without me. It's been rough on all of us lately. "I see what you're doing, Kingston."

He chuckles and kisses me again. "Is it working?"

"Better than you know."

He gently sets me on my feet and crosses the room to the closet. "Good. I plan to keep it that way. Now time to get dressed. We have plans."

I hug myself. "Please don't tell me I have to make my appearance."

He scrunches his face and flicks through the hangers. "Okay, I won't tell you. But don't worry. Not until later."

"Really?"

He unhooks a black one-piece garment from its hanger and holds it out with a frown. "This isn't exactly sexy, and I never imagined I'd want you to wear so many clothes, but I want you to stay warm."

I twist my lips, giving the body suit a once-over. He was right about it not being cute. "Why do I have to wear this?"

"We'll be outside."

"Outside?"

He heaves a dramatic breath and closes the space between us. Hooking his fingers to the hem of my shirt, he bunches it between his hands. "No more questions. You're going to drag the surprise right out of me."

Before I can ask him about the surprise, he tugs my shirt over my head incredibly fast and presses his chest to mine, making me laugh. But I don't get a chance to enjoy his skin against me for more than a second. He steps back and hands me a long-sleeved shirt.

"Hurry up before I get distracted," he murmurs.

"I like your distractions," I tease.

He groans under his breath and closes his eyes. "Get dressed. Now. I'm fucking begging you."

I snort and cover my mouth with my hand. "Say please and maybe—"

Kingston rushes me, making me squeal. Lifting me off my feet, he drops me onto the bed and lies on top of me, using his hand to spread my legs so he can rest between them.

"Fuck it. No surprise for you," he murmurs, closing the space to kiss me. "All the distractions instead."

I hold my hand up and block his mouth. "Maybe if you tell me."

"Nope. Not happening," he mumbles against my skin before licking my palm to get me to pull away. "Which is too bad. Because I think you'd have liked it."

I giggle and poke his nose. "Aw, dude. Come on."

He presses his weight into me, resting his head above my shoulder. "Nope. This is your life now. Forever under me. Maybe on the side sometimes. Most definitely on top."

"It's a good thing I like it."

Kingston laughs loudly at my quip. "Fucking A. I love you, babe, but you need to be careful. I take your desires seriously. I told you I'm fully prepared to spend eternity in bed with you."

I crack up and pat his chest, nudging him up. "You're bad."

"Well, you did put me on the naughty list."

Kingston snaps his teeth at me and kisses me once more before relenting to pull me back to my feet. I'm actually surprised he does. But then I hear Austin and Diego murmuring from the living room and realize that they're waiting on us.

"Because you deserved it, you know," I tease a little late, letting him help me step into the body suit.

Kingston hands me a pair of pants to put on top of it, and then a sweater and jacket. By the time he wraps the scarf around my neck, slides the gloves over my fingers, and adjusts a knit beanie over my hair, I can barely move.

He steps away from me and crosses his arms. "I hate it."

"I can't move well. It's a little hot too."

"And not the good kind."

I laugh and swat his shoulder. "Then maybe you should just help me undre—"

Kingston cuts me off with a heavy sigh. "Don't even finish your words. I have no restraint today, and I'll never hear the end of it from my brothers if we don't stick to the plan. But you bet I'm going to count down the time until later.

You and me on that bed, giving in to all the distractions."

"We'll see," I say, patting his cheek.

He releases a fake growl.

"I was thinking the couch looked pretty comfortable too."

Releasing a loud, exaggerated groan, he closes his eyes and nudges me toward the door. "Get moving. Seriously. I can't take this."

When I open the door, I catch sight of Diego and Austin sitting on the couch. They're as bundled up as I am, wearing heavy jackets and beanies. I offer each of them a smile as I cross the room. Kingston grumbles the whole time he changes in the room about how many hours until he gets me alone again, and I shake my head and open my arms to invite Diego and Austin into them.

"If you want us to make additional plans, just say the word, beautiful," Diego says, grinning at me. "We'll gladly keep you busy. We know how wound up Kingston gets during the holidays."

"It's only now," Kingston says, coming up behind me.

I spin to face him. "Why's that?"

"Because of you," Austin says.

"Me?"

Kingston disappears from in front of me and clocks him in the arm. "Shut up, Austin."

Diego slides his arm over my shoulders and guides me away. "Kingston's afraid you'll get freaked out by everything, but I think you can handle it."

"You hope," Kingston mutters.

"Our girl is badass. No hope needed."

Before the two of them start arguing, Austin offers his hand out to me and tugs me toward the front door to the cabin. Kingston and Diego quickly follow his lead and beat us there. Diego cracks the door open and peeks outside, and Kingston wags his eyebrows at me and extends his hand for me to hold with my free one.

A gust of icy wind blows in through the crack, and Diego stands tall, blocking my view of the night. "Close your eyes, beautiful."

I purse my lips. "Really?"

Austin lets go of my hand to slide behind me, placing his palms over my eyes to block my view. Kingston tugs me forward, and Diego links his fingers through my hand that Austin let go. I can't stop the smile crossing my lips at their anticipation. It's better than even the thought of a holiday surprise. I don't care what it is, because being sandwiched between them is better than any present.

"Walk slowly and carefully," Kingston says.

The second I shuffle forward, my feet slip out right from under me. I scream as I fall back into Austin too quickly for him to catch and for Kingston and Diego to stop. We hit the ground together with me on top of Austin. He laughs from beneath me, tightening his hold across my stomach, not even trying to help me up.

I inhale a few deep breaths of icy air in surprise. "Holy shit balls. What the hell happened?"

"You didn't listen to me about being careful and slipped," Kingston says from above me.

"Obviously," I say, rolling my eyes. "But on what? I've never felt anything like it."

No one responds to me, but Kingston's face lights up with a smile that competes with the one Diego gives me. I don't even have to look at Austin to know he's smiling as well.

"Sit up and look, babe," Kingston finally says. "It's the first part of your surprise."

Austin bends forward, propping himself up with me, and I stare at the world in front of us. The twinkling lights illuminate rainbow colors across the white ground, sparkling unlike anything I've ever seen.

"Oh, shit," I say, my mouth dropping open. "Snow?"

Kingston chuckles. "Apparently the universe heard our wish to make this the best holiday for you."

I scramble to my feet and nearly slip and fall again on the icy walkway. If it wasn't for Austin hooking his fingers to my hips, I'd land in the fresh, untouched snow outside our door. "I can't believe it. This is real, right?"

Diego bends down and scoops a handful up and tosses it into the air. The freezing snow sprinkles across my cheeks, making me shiver before melting against the warmth of my skin. "Cool, isn't it? We didn't even have to arrange any snow machines."

"Snow machines? You can do that?"

He bobs his head. "It's the Days of The Divide. We can do whatever we want."

BLOOD HOLIDAY

THE WORLD BLURS AROUND ME, and Diego hollers a laugh and grips onto my waist to keep me firmly between his legs. My stomach rises into my chest at the sudden drop, cutting off the sounds trying to escape my mouth. He shifts his weight, leaning right, and Austin comes into view at the bottom of the hill.

"Watch out!" I manage to yell as Diego leans the other way, purposely aiming to send us flying toward Austin.

He accepts Diego's game of dare and extends his arms wide. "Brace yourself, Jewel. I got you."

Kingston appears next to him and shoves him back.

"No, you don't. She's mine next."

"Shit, no." Diego roars a laugh again, jerking our bodies the other way.

Austin rushes to get back in our path, now running toward us in a blur. Kingston collides into his back, sending him face first into the snow. The two of them disappear in a fight I can't keep up with. Diego tightens his arms around me, leaning more to direct us toward a break in the trees.

Both Kingston and Austin stop and block our way, flashing their fangs.

"Ah, fuck," I say, squeezing my eyes shut as I brace myself for a game of keep away.

Diego throws the both of us sideways into the snow, sending the empty sled at his brothers. Skidding across the snow, Diego holds me on top of him, and we slip and slide a few feet. We jostle and jerk to a stop. Snow explodes around us, engulfing us in a cloud of white.

"Fucking Diego! You could've killed Jewel!" Kingston shouts. "Babe, you okay?"

I gasp a breath and release a loud ass laugh, swiping the freezing snow from my face. "That was friggin' awesome!"

Diego rolls me off him into the snow, chuckling. He raises his hand, and we high-five each other. "Hell yeah, it was."

"You could've been hurt," Kingston says, stomping

through the snow toward us.

Austin appears by my side. "Are you?"

I dig my hands into the snow and throw it at the both of them. "Would I be laughing if I was?"

Kingston shakes the snow from his messy hair. "I don't know. You sometimes laugh at the weirdest times."

I throw another handful of snow at him. "Says the guy who laughs every single time I—"

Kingston flies at me and plants his cold lips to mine, shutting me up. I laugh and press my hands to his chest, and Diego shoves him sideways and into the snow. I screech at the sudden flurry of snowballs whizzing past me, and Austin opens his jacket to shield me. I crawl closer and sneak my hands around his back, letting him zipper me inside with him.

"Told you I'd get you," he whispers, hovering his mouth an inch from mine without kissing me.

I don't even get the chance to make my move before a mound of snow falls on our heads and into Austin's jacket. He's quick to unzip us as the snow turns into ice water to soak through his sweater. I rub my hands up and down his chest, making him smile.

"Austin's going to be fine, babe," Kingston says, coming up beside me. "Me, on the other hand..."

I turn toward him, my eyes wide. "Shit, you're turning

blue."

Diego drops more snow on Kingston. "He'll survive."

Kingston puckers out his bottom lip in the most adorably ridiculous pout I've ever seen, and I can't resist closing the space to him. His teeth chatter and he shivers, and I can't tell whether he's being dramatic or not, but I decide to play his game.

Unzipping my jacket, I hold it open. "Come here, Kingston. I'll warm you up."

Diego raises his eyebrows. "Damn it."

Austin shakes his head. "You know how our girl can't resist taking care of us."

Kingston clenches his teeth, surely stopping a wide grin from plastering on his face. He snakes his hands around my waist, sliding into my arms so that I can hug him. "I think I'm ready to go back. You can stay here with Diego and Austin if you want."

I nuzzle my cold nose to his freezing one. "I am a little cold. Plus it's your night."

"Don't forget we have to meet Mitchell in an hour," Diego says.

Kingston groans. "Fuck."

"Can't you tell him I'm sick again?" I ask, sticking out my bottom lip to mirror Kingston's expression.

"Yes," Kingston says at the same time both Austin and

Diego say, "No."

The three of them glower at each other.

"Tonight's important, beautiful. You'll be fine. It's just a dinner and the gift exchange."

My mouth forms an O. "Oh, no. You guys didn't tell me we'd be exchanging gifts."

"It's not what you think," Kingston says. "Promise. No one expects you to give anyone anything."

"And you give us plenty, Jewel," Austin says, smiling.

"But I can think of something special you can give me now," Kingston adds, snuggling his face into my neck.

I laugh and pat his cheek. Leaning close, I press my lips to his ear so that only he can hear me. "But we only have an hour."

He moans deep in his throat. "Shit, then we better hurry."

Kingston scoops me off my feet, making me laugh so loudly that I'm sure every nearby vampire can hear me. He shouts to his brothers that we might be late and practically flies us through the dark night and back to the glowing cabin.

Warm air wraps around me the second we enter and Kingston slows down. He strategically shifts me in his arms, adjusting my legs to wrap around his hips. Even through all the extra layers of clothing, I can feel every impressive inch of him.

"Can I undress you?" he asks, setting me on the edge of the bed. "I've been dying for a moment alone with you all night."

"Is that so?" I ask.

"While I like hanging out with my brothers, I much prefer to do so on their nights with you."

"Of course you do," I tease. "And before you complain any more, did you forget you're the one who invited them."

"We always spend the holidays together."

"You spend every day together too," I muse.

"Only since meeting you."

"Well, I love it. I miss it—I mean, the closeness I used to have with Ramona." I swallow, my throat suddenly burning at the thought. "I'm happy that this works for us. Because I love you all."

He smiles and sits next to me on the bed, twining our fingers together. "I know it's not always easy being with us, but—"

"It's the easiest thing I've ever done in my life."

His whole face lights up with my words, and he cups his cold fingers to my face to kiss me, not giving me a second longer to think about my life before. I sink against him, kissing him deeper, wanting nothing more than to explore our body match. With everything that's happened the last few weeks, we've unintentionally pulled back from each other to deal with the mess Brayla created of my life. But I don't want space anymore. I don't want Kingston to coddle me and do everything he can to assure I always smile. I just want to be with him. Feel him. Enjoy him and how much he craves me.

Unzipping his jacket, I rush to get it off of him, making him laugh as I yank his arms up to get it out of the way. I hook my fingers to his sweater next and continue to undress him. He grins and shifts, watching me drink in the sight of him without his shirt for a moment. And then I unclasp the button on his pants, sending his heart racing.

"I should be the one undressing you," he murmurs, lifting his hips so that I can tug his pants down.

I pause, admiring his tight muscles and the V of his hips that disappear into his boxer-briefs. "Then why aren't you?"

He releases a breathless laugh and wiggles his fingers, motioning for me to close the space between us. For once, he doesn't rush to rip my clothes off, taking a torturous amount of time to peel off every layer of clothing to pile with his on the floor.

"I've missed you," he whispers, shifting me onto his lap when the only clothes remaining on me are my undergarments.

"I'm sorry," I say. "I know I haven't been exactly easy.

It's just—"

Bringing his mouth to mine, he silences my explanation and kisses me until he's certain I won't continue. "None of that now. What matters is that you're here and with me, and I'm dying to be with you if you let me."

I nod. "I want nothing more."

Kingston reacts to my words with a kiss that steals my breath away. His tongue brushes over mine, and he works his hands over me, unhooking my bra before rolling me over to finish undressing me. He pulls the warm blankets around us, blocking out the world, and all I can focus on are his dark eyes capturing mine in their intensity.

I open myself completely to him, feeling the weight of his body sink down on mine until he's between my legs. I gasp at the good pressure, clinging onto him while his lips meet mine again, muffling the soft moans that quickly turn desperate. He breaks away, kissing over my jaw, sliding his hand under my ass to pull me even closer.

Not once does he mention the healed bite mark Austin gave me, his own focus drawn to my lips against his, my hands combing through his hair, my body warming his. Tingles build through me with his motions, his hands travel-ing over my skin, leaving my body buzzing until I feel like I'm going to burst. He kisses me a dozen times more as I shudder through the sudden release that sends me pressing my body deeper into the bed. Kingston slows, a smile on his face, and he lies on top of me just feeling my heart crash against his as they attempt to be together.

He frames my head with his elbows, resting his forehead to mine. "I'm pretty damn sure we're skipping the party."

I nuzzle my nose to his. "But you were looking forward to it."

He raises an eyebrow. "Was not."

"You can't fool me, Kingston."

"I'm serious. Maybe if..." He lets his words trail off. "It's just—you don't celebrate it. And I'm pretty sure you might never want to."

I pull away to bring his face into focus. "I don't care if it doesn't mean anything to me, even when I turn. But what I care about is what it means to you. And while I know it's some weird rise of the vampire celebration, that's not what it truly is to you. It's about hanging out with your family. With people you love."

"I wouldn't take it that far," he teases. "Maybe if it was just us Divines."

"I'm going to pretend it is," I say, smiling.

"Please do."

I scrunch my nose. "Unless they start devouring people."

He yanks the blanket over our heads and tightens his

arms around me. "Okay, never mind. We're definitely not going."

My eyes widen. "Wait, they do that?"

"We survive on blood, so..."

I try not to react, because I can't tell if he's joking or not. "So it's a bloody holiday."

"But we're going to make it more. For you, babe."

"How?"

"You'll see."

HOLIDAY CHEER

THREE SOFT INTAKES OF BREATH sound through the air the moment I step from the walk-in closet. I smile and adjust the long skirt of my deep red gown that matches perfectly with the ruby bracelet I found tucked among my belongings.

"You were right," Austin says, elbowing Kingston.

"Ravishing in red," he responds, smiling at me. "Perfect."

Diego leans in closer to his brothers and whispers, "Also perfect for when she ravages me later. I don't know why you don't ask her to bite back. Fucking hot as hell."

I place my hands on my hips and raise my eyebrows. The three of them laugh. Austin and Diego bump fists, and Kingston flashes his fangs at me in a wide smile, sending warmth flushing across my skin at the memory of our time together.

"You know I can hear you all whispering, right?" I say, stepping forward. "And Diego, what happened to not giving details?"

"It only applies to asking you, and you're supposed to give us some pretend privacy, babe," Kingston says.

Diego crosses the room and opens his arms for me. "Sorry, beautiful. I won't do it again."

I rest my head to his chest for a moment. "It's fine as long as you all don't start fighting."

"You don't have to worry about that with me," Kingston says. "Those blunt, bitey teeth of yours can stick to Diego."

Austin comes up behind me and rests his chin to my shoulder. "Maybe me too if you want."

OhmyeffingGod. My body shudders at his whispered words, reacting beyond my control at the memory of our intimate moment of exploring our nutrients match. I suck in a small breath, closing my eyes. "Ah hell," I murmur, trying to get my body to control itself.

Kingston groans. "Damn it. What did you say to her? I

need her to react to me like that."

I lick my lips. "Don't even, Austin."

He chuckles and slides his fingers into my hair to push it out of the way from my back. He kisses the nape of my neck. "Wasn't going to. I don't have the urge to brag like my brothers. I like to keep our amazing moments to myself."

A smile creeps across my face, and I spin in his arms to face him.

"Damn it," Kingston repeats. "Austin, we're in this together."

I wag my finger behind me to get Kingston to stop. "Sometimes it's okay to keep things apart. I love what I have with each of you, dude."

"But I want what they have," he complains.

Austin flies away from me at his brother, and the two of them collide to the floor. Neither of them gets in any punches that I can see, but the coffee table cracks and splits in half. I can't tell who crashed into it.

"Guys, really?" I ask, shifting on my feet, trying to follow their movement to see if I can intervene.

Diego scoops me up and spins me around. "I don't think so, beautiful."

I press my hands to his chest. "But someone will get hurt."

Swiveling again, he shifts me out of the way as Austin

and Kingston fly by. "And I'm assuring it won't be you. They need to work it out themselves."

The two of them suddenly stop, and I frown at the fact that Austin has Kingston in a headlock. Kingston tries to swing his fist into Austin's stomach, but Austin moves behind him and holds him in place.

"Oh, come on," I say. "You two are being ridiculous."

"Sorry, Jewel," Austin says. "I'm not going to stand here and let him pressure you."

"I wasn't going to. I just wanted to know what I could do to make things even more satisfying for our girl. Kill me for wanting that."

"I considered it," Austin grumbles.

The door to the cabin swings open, startling me with a gust of icy air. The four of us were too focused on each other that we didn't hear Mitchell approach. He stands in the doorway, a sprinkling of snow covering his hat, and then he gives each of his sons a pointed look.

"Is everything okay in here?" he asks, thankfully loud enough for me to hear.

"Yeah, fucking great," Kingston mutters.

Mitchell strolls into the room and shuts the door behind him. Dusting the snow from his coat, he narrows his gaze on me, giving me a once-over that has my hands automatically gripping onto Diego. Mitchell hasn't once mentioned anything about my sister or the Blood Rebels he massacred, and it freaks me out how well he pretends he totally didn't betray my guys.

But we can't do anything. It would be unfair of me to ask my guys to. Mitchell is their dad, and everything we have comes from his Divine name. At least I don't have to like the guy.

Extending his hand to me, Mitchell offers me a smile. "You look spectacular, Jewel. A beauty as exquisite as your name."

Damn, the man can give a compliment. And eff my stupid mouth for betraying my mind and smiling at his words.

"Thanks," I manage to say, keeping my voice even though my insides scream.

He turns to his sons. "It's not a wonder she has you three riled up. But might I remind you that now's not the time to turn against each other. I expect better from you, especially when the time comes for her to choose." His voice sounds out annoyingly low so that I shouldn't be able to hear him.

If only my damn heart didn't react.

"She's the best thing I've ever seen," Diego says, kissing my cheek. His quick gesture and verbal response to Mitchell's compliment before he warned them stops the reaction my mouth wants to give Mitchell.

"And you don't have to worry about us," Kingston whispers, responding to Mitchell's comment about them. "We're not fighting. Just partaking in a friendly competition. You can't expect us not to enjoy every ounce of her affection while we still can."

Mitchell squeezes his shoulder. "I hope so, son. It's of utmost importance that you three remember your place as a Divine."

Kingston side-glances me. "And Jewel will know hers."

"Very good." Mitchell turns to me again, taking a moment to drift his gaze to the vow pendant around my neck. "Are you ready, my dear? The others are quite excited to see you again."

Doubt it but okay.

I bob my head, trying my best to act cheerful, though Kingston's words to Mitchell stir fear inside me. My place? I grew up thinking I knew my place in the world. I accepted the donor life. But now? The only place I know I belong is by my guys' sides, but it sounds like Mitchell might have another idea.

"Hopefully not too excited," Diego says, twining his fingers through mine. "We don't want to have to excuse ourselves early."

"I assure you that everyone will be on their best behavior." Mitchell eyes me again like he directs his words at me.

I respond with a smile and let Kingston take me from Diego to lead me out behind Mitchell. Austin stays close to my back, draping a warm shawl over my shoulders before the freezing air has a chance to seep into my bones. Diego falls in place at Mitchell's side to stay in front. I don't even get a chance to step into the snow before Kingston picks me up, sneakily hiking up my dress in the process to wrap my legs around him. He speeds to the grand glass and wood mansion so fast that my body doesn't have the chance to shiver.

"Mr. Divines, what an honor it is to finally have you join us," a familiar feminine voice says. "Mitchell said your match was feeling ill. I do hope that isn't a frequent occurrence. Her health is rather important. We wouldn't want her heirs to question your ability to—"

"Jewel's in impeccable health," Austin says, cutting off Viorica Vaduva, one of two female vampires on the Donor Life Corp board. "I guarantee it."

"I feel great," I say. I can't help it. "The Divines take the best care of me."

She turns her gaze to me for the first time. If I hadn't said anything, she'd have ignored my presence altogether, one of the sometimes annoying things vampires do, but then again, it's terrifying when they don't. The only vampiric attention I want is from my guys.

"You'll inform the board if things change, correct? We wouldn't want you to be unhappy in your arrangement. Others have vocally stated an interest in you."

"Where are your daughters anyway?" Kingston says, peering around the brightly lit room. "I want nothing more than to avoid them."

"I'm sure you won't have that problem seeing as they agree."

I can't stop myself from hanging onto every word. My guys once mentioned that some of Viorica's daughters applied to Blood Match with me, and they're bitter they didn't make it very far.

Soft voices murmur from a grand archway, and all of us turn our attention in that direction. Someone calls Viorica's name, and she disappears without a word. Vampire social norms always confuse the hell out of me. Sometimes they'll greet each other and offer pleasantries and other times they won't even acknowledge anyone's existence.

Kingston slides his fingers through mine and brings my hand to his mouth to kiss. "Why don't we get this over with so we can head back to our cabin as soon as possible?"

Diego links his fingers to my free hand. "I have our whole day planned. Movies in bed until we can't keep our eyes open, followed by breakfast, maybe a drive through the mountainside?"

"Don't forget the gift exchange," Kingston says. "I've worked incredibly hard on my present to Jewel."

I furrow my brows. "No more presents. I can't even get you anything."

"What did I say?" Kingston asks, grinning at me. "You're enough."

"And so are you," I say. "All of you. Though, I might need you all to join me in the tub again later to relax."

"Only if you forgo the bikini," Kingston murmurs. "And the bubbles."

I laugh. "I will if you will."

"Done."

"I meant all of you."

He grumbles at me and shakes his head. "That sounds far from fun."

I laugh. "I don't know. It sounds like the best idea ever."

Diego laughs. "Come on, Kingston. You don't want to deny our girl."

Austin smirks at me. "I'll do whatever you want."

I blink a few times. "Shit. I—"

Kingston tips his head back and laughs. "Okay, we'll talk about this later, and only because I like seeing our girl blush."

"Fuck. Me. What am I getting myself into?" I murmur

mostly to myself.

"A good time," Kingston quips. "And only because it's the holidays. You deserve all the holiday cheer."

"No, babe. You're sitting with us." Kingston intercepts me before I automatically head toward the table with a massive amount of food. I've never seen so much at once. Even when the chefs at the Blood Match Center go all out for me, those mini buffets look like scraps in comparison to this.

"But there are chairs there, and I eat solids, remember?" I say, eyeing the colorful collection of foods on tray warmers. I have no idea what some of the stuff is, but it smells delicious.

"Did you not feed Jewel?" Austin asks, backhanding Kingston on the arm. "You have to remember to feed her, asshole. She doesn't always speak up."

I raise an eyebrow at him, and Austin's cheeks flush, blooming red.

"I mean...I'm sorry. I didn't mean to make you sound like a pet Kingston forgot to care for."

I giggle and touch his cheek. "It's fine, Austin. I know you're just assuring I get what I need."

"That's why he's your nutrients match," Diego says, knocking his fist to Austin's arm.

"And why I'm your body match. I do plenty fine assuring that our girl gets everything else she needs for that sexy ass body of hers."

Laughter from the doorway draws my attention from my guys, and I gape at the line of all-male humans talking amongst themselves as they head into the room. None of them bow their heads toward the floor like the human staff of the Divinity Estate, and I can't help gawking as they all take seats at the table of food Diego now stands tall in front of, obviously attempting to block my view.

"Please don't tell me they're being prepped for donations," I say, leaning to try to peer around my hulking personality match.

Austin stands too close, not letting me sneak a peek. "No, they're part of the gift exchange."

I swing my head to peer at him, my brows puckering. "What?"

"The gift exchange. The one I told you no one expects you to be a part of, babe," Kingston says.

"You give humans to each other?" I ask, failing to lower my voice. "Don't most of the human staffs have family? What about their contracts?"

"Jewel, try to stay calm," Austin whispers. "Most aren't being forced against their wills. They volunteer for the added bonus. The majority of them don't have family, or if they do, they're more interested in starting new ones."

Diego points to a familiar man sitting at the end of the table not even hiding the fact that we're discussing him. The man lifts his hand and waves at Diego. I recognize him from the gardening staff of the Divinity Estate. He always picked the best flowers for me since I enjoy having them in our rooms. "Gerald entered and won the transfer lottery this year. We've arranged to give him to the Monroe Region so that he could sign a donor union with someone on staff at the Townsend Chateau."

"Oh," I murmur. "I guess that was nice."

A man with long, blond hair jumps up across from Gerald and yells out. Just as quickly, a vampire materializes behind him and forces him back in his seat. No one else at the table reacts. Then the vampire, who glances to me for a split second with his fangs flashing, leans in and captures the guy in his stare.

"What the?"

"Come on, let's take our seats, babe," Kingston says, draping his arm over my shoulders to pull me away.

"But—"

"Babe, please. I'm begging you."

"He looks like—"

It's Diego who spins me toward him and plants his lips to mine, stealing the argument from me before I can say it out loud. It's then that my guys' words swirl through my mind again, and I realize that Austin said *most* humans volunteer. Not all. The guy who jumped up must be in the latter category.

My stomach knots at the thought, but I give in and let Diego's big hands smooth the nerves from me. If it weren't for my guys surrounding me and doing their best to keep me away, I might have said something I couldn't take back. Something that could've messed this all up. I might be a Blood Match to the Divines, but in the eyes of other vampires, I'm still a donor.

"Babe, we can go," Kingston whispers. "I'm not going to force you to stay because of what Mitchell wants."

"We can rotate, so we're still all present," Austin adds.

Diego rests his head to mine. "Agree. This was a bad idea."

"But this is your holiday," I say, squeaking the words out. "It's part of your life and tradition." And it's utterly and completely unfair to make them break something that they've bonded over for longer than I can grasp. "I just need a moment to process. I promised you all forever, and if this is what it entails, then I'll learn to accept it."

The three of them engulf me in a group hug that leaves me laughing. With their reaction, I'd think that I somehow had given them a holiday miracle or something. Maybe I have. I know they worry about what I think about their lives.

About the vampire life.

"Because you're my future," I add, taking a moment to kiss each of them.

"And you're ours," they all say, making me smile again.

"As long as you remember to feed me," I tease.

Diego howls a laugh and whacks Kingston on the back. "You know I will. Any way you want."

"Let's start with something from that amazing looking buffet over there." I motion to the humans murmuring with excitement while they eat. "And we'll save the other stuff for later."

"Or we can sneak out for a moment now," Kingston murmurs. "Because, fuck."

Austin winks at me. "You make us rather starved."

THE GIFT EXCHANGE

"THIS IS SO AWKWARD," I whisper into Kingston's ear.

"Wouldn't be if you'd squirm a little more," he says back, kissing the base of my throat.

I shift my ass on his lap for a second and slide off him to sit on the bench between him and Diego. "Not helping, dude."

"Oh, but I can."

I giggle and climb over Diego to sit between him and Austin. Diego leans forward and blocks Kingston's attempt to tug me back over to him. They both glare at each other and then laugh.

Turning in his seat, Mitchell meets our gazes. "Shhh. Some of us want to watch the show."

And by show, he means the shit show parade of human men posing in front of us with big red and green bows slung across their chests, all grinning in their undergarments. Except for the one man on the end. He sadly stands there like a zombie under his current mister's mind manipulation.

"Sorry," Kingston says, sticking his tongue out at me.

Mitchell shakes his head and turns around, leaning back on the table.

Soft, upbeat music starts and the lights dim around us while one beams across the table the humans stand on like a makeshift stage. Each of them holds an envelope in their hands with the region they're being given to hidden inside. The tradition is based on what Austin referred to as Secret Santa.

And from all the smiling vampires, flashing their sharp fangs in a strangely friendly way I've never seen anyone show each other apart from how my guys look at each other and me, I can tell that the anticipation is killing them.

Diego slides his fingers over my leg while Austin links his fingers through mine. Kingston's hand rubs between my shoulders as he crowds Diego, but neither of them says anything to each other. And I suddenly feel a wave of excitement wash over me. Not because of the weirdest friggin' tradition I have ever learned about but because I get to experience a piece of my guys' lives, something I know is hard for them to do but hope they'll come around to.

A vampire man, wearing a stylish red suit with a white tie, steps in front of the table and grins at the crowd. "Welcome to the annual Mount Crescent gift exchange!"

"What a spectacle," I whisper under my breath.

"Great, right?" Kingston says, playing with my hair.

Not exactly the words I was thinking, but I wouldn't dare steal his Days of The Divide cheer no matter how I feel about it. My dad would flip his shit if... I push the thought away. I still can't think about him or what happened to him. Brayla either.

"Tonight, we have a delectable selection of the finest donors from across the regions," the vampire says.

"Doubtful," Kingston murmurs.

Austin leans into me. "No one actually gives away the best."

I purse my lips. "I don't know. I'm going to miss Gerald. He always picked the prettiest flowers."

"Without even having been told," Austin says.

I raise my eyebrows. "Really?"

"Don't tell her that, bro. You'll make her sad." Diego brings his hand up from my leg to lace our fingers together.

I shake my head. "No, I'm okay. If this is what he wanted."

The music suddenly grows louder, and I cringe as it steals away all other noise. None of the other vampires react, and I try to play off my reaction as having a crick in my neck. I press my head into Diego's shoulder, attempting to muffle the noise. Kingston's hand slides up my back and into my hair, and he stretches and covers my other ear with his hand in a way no one could see under my hair.

And then the dancing begins.

I tip my head back and laugh so loudly that everyone turns and looks in my direction. Gerald smiles at me from his spot on the table and waves his envelope back and forth in the same rhythm of his hips.

All three of my guys chuckle at my reaction, and I laugh even harder. I can't stop either. This was nothing like I expected from a human gift exchange. I mean, mostly everyone seems to be enjoying themselves. It's like the holiday season turned some of the world's most vicious predators into snow bunnies, dazzled with the magic of back-world decorations.

"You wanna dance, beautiful?" Diego asks, tipping his head to mine.

"Now?" I peer around. "No one else is."

He swirls his finger at the makeshift stage. "I see plenty of people dancing."

I don't get a chance to respond before Diego lifts me

right off the bench and sets me on my feet. I've never felt so awkward in my life as Diego spins me around, but then Austin joins us and grins at me with the biggest smile I've ever seen on him. Kingston plops a Santa hat on my head and chuckles, completing their circle around me, making it easy to forget the strange vampire customs and what the night is all about.

"Perhaps Jewel would like to announce the revelations," Mitchell says from his spot, talking over the music.

I peek around Austin at him. "The revelations?"

"It's an honor to be chosen for such an occasion, Ms. Divine," Gerald says from his spot, still dancing with his envelope. "I'd love you to present me to my new region, though I'll always cherish being a Divine."

I pause in my dancing and peer at the other vampires. Viorica presses her lips together and raises an eyebrow, daring me to turn this weird ass opportunity down. It's written all over her face.

"Um, okay. I guess I can." Stupid squeaky voice.

Nerves threaten to steal away the warmth the moment of dancing with my guys brought on.

"Come on, babe. I'll help you," Kingston says, smirking at me.

Picking me off my feet, he zooms me to the table with the humans. He sets me on the bench, giving me a view of the grand dining hall. I swallow the burning in my throat and wet my lips, feeling the weight of more than a dozen eyes on me. The vampire in the red suit has the nerve to wink, and Kingston shifts in front of me like he just realized how much attention falls in our direction. Unwanted attention at that.

The music lowers, and I immediately regret agreeing to this crap. Friggin' Mitchell. It's like he purposely put me on the spot as a test. My guys warned me that after our run-in with the Blood Rebels that Mitchell might pull shit like this. And he used the festivities to disguise the fact that he's gauging my worth to be a Divine.

"All you have to do is announce the human and open the envelope," Kingston whispers.

I bob my head and dart my eyes over the room, finding Austin and Diego standing nearby. They both smile at me, giving me the strength to pull myself together to get through this even with my heart racing out of control.

My hand trembles as I extend it out to Gerald and take his envelope. Clearing my throat, I say, "I hope everyone's been enjoying the festivities tonight."

A few vampires, including Viorica, Mitchell, and a silver-haired dude that I can't remember his name, smile at me and nod.

"You don't have to make a speech, babe," Kingston

whispers.

I blush. "You sure? Everyone looks like I need to wish them the friggin' bloodiest holiday."

Kingston flashes his fangs at me in a smile. "Only me."

"We don't have all night, Ms. Divine," Viorica says from her spot. She crosses her legs and leans back on the table.

"You kind of do," I mutter under my breath. "That's why you're celebrating."

Kingston roars a laugh, far too amused by this whole situation. "Okay, okay. Now you need to hurry before you add a bunch more enemies to our list."

"You said you'd help me," I whisper.

Faking a sigh, Kingston steps onto the bench beside me. "All right. We'll make this quick. First up is a donor from the Divinity Estate, well-built and active, skilled in all things daylight-household related, and interested in procreation."

It takes everything in me not to react to his comment.

"And this alluring human will now transfer to..." Kingston motions for me to tear the envelope.

I swipe my finger through it and pull out the small card and hold it out. "The Townsend Chateau in the Monroe Region."

The silver-haired vampire hops to his feet and shakes Mitchell's hand. A second later, both he and Gerald disappear so quickly that I don't even get the chance to say good-bye. A few other vampires disperse, and I realize that they might have been part of the silver-haired vampire's coven. I guess only their exchange matters to them.

"All right. Next up is a strong, well-educated donor from the Flannigan Region. He...looks like he might be feisty." Kingston motions for me to grab the envelope from the man at the end, who stares off into space. "And easily compliant. He'll find his new home with..."

I tug the envelope free from his death grip and turn back toward the vampires to read the card inside. "Looks like this guy's going to Midnight Valley in the Vaduva Regio—"

Something heavy hits my back, and the world blurs around me. I topple off the bench and scream. But I don't slam into the floor. Kingston hooks his hands to my waist and yanks me away from the man midair, who suddenly came to his senses, and he crashes to the floor at our feet. Hollering, he thrashes his body and scrambles in an attempt to fight off anyone who comes near him. But no one moves.

The man gets to his feet, his eyes wildly darting around, searching his surroundings. "Come any closer, and you'll regret it."

No one takes the guy seriously, and the vampires start to murmur like he didn't just try to tackle me.

"I think you'll regret it more if you don't settle down,"

Kingston says. "You're lucky I'm in a good mood or else—"

Glass shatters, spraying across the floor. I don't even have time to move before something blurs through the room and grabs the man. His yells disappear with him, and I'm left frozen in shock, staring into the snowy, dark night outside the broken window.

And then my world blurs.

UNINVITED

ICY AIR WRAPS AROUND ME for a split second before I'm engulfed in warmth. Cold lips brush against mine, and I heave a breath into Kingston's mouth, trying to orient myself to the sudden relocation. Dizziness washes over me, and he jerks back to sit me on the couch.

Austin kneels in front of me and cups my cheeks to peer into my eyes. "Just take a slow breath."

I swallow and tilt my chin to my chest, doing as he says. Diego sits down next to me and holds up a glass of water to my lips. I slowly sip, letting the room temperature water coat my tongue for a moment.

"What h-happened?" I manage to ask, my voice crack-ing.

"It seems that we had an uninvited guest," Kingston says, tapping his finger on his phone. "It happens, especially in remote areas like this."

"We were probably followed up the mountain," Diego says. "But don't worry, beautiful. You're safe. We won't let anything happen to you. The trespasser will be taken care of any moment."

"You sure?" I ask, meeting his stormy gaze.

Austin pulls himself onto the couch next to me and rubs his hand across my shoulder blades. "If he's not, he won't stick around."

Kingston rocks on his heels and glances toward the door. "Yeah, he already got what he wanted."

I groan, covering my face with my hands. That poor man. It's one thing for those humans who volunteered to be part of the gift exchange, but that man clearly didn't want to. And now? He's facing an unimaginable fate by the hands of a starved vampire. My stomach clenches at the thought.

"So if he's already gone, then that's it?" My voice comes out so softly that I'm not even sure I said the words out loud.

"Sorry, babe," Kingston says. "This is why we were hesi-tant to—"

I drop my hands to look at him. "This can't be it."

"I don't want to upset you, beautiful, but the chances of him surviving aren't good." Diego takes my hand into his. "I'm sorry."

"Can you at least check? If he's still out there, maybe—"

"You want us to hunt the guy?" Kingston asks. "That would require us to separate. If there is one uninvited guest, there might be more. They'll attempt to steal the rest of the humans here, and I guarantee no one will put up that much of a fight. Losing one human—"

Austin shoves Kingston in the gut, sending him back a foot. "You're going to upset her."

"I'm just being honest," he mutters. "She needs to know the danger and what we're doing to protect her."

"You're forgetting about something," Diego says. "Her heart. Look at her. Jewel told us that this is the time of year that humans fear. Doing nothing will ruin it."

Resting my elbows on my knees, I slump forward, trying to process everything. I don't mean to react like I do, but sitting here, trying to pretend that shadow dwellers aren't taking the whole Days of The Divide seriously as they claim what they want, doesn't sit right with me. Why am I the only one worthy of protection? *Because you're a future Divine Heir.*

"So what do you want to do?" Kingston asks Diego.

"I'm not leaving our girl. Not for—"

A loud wail cuts through the air, drawing our attention to the door. Austin and Diego hop up, and Kingston scoops me into his arms and holds me against his chest. Growls sound out from outside the cabin, and glass shatters.

"Help!" a familiar, masculine voice yells. "Please, someone help!"

I push against the solid wall of muscle Diego creates. "That's Gerald!"

Kingston covers my mouth with his hand. "Babe, please. You have to be quiet."

"But—"

Austin turns around to peer into my watery eyes. "Jewel, I need you to listen carefully. I'll go after Gerald, but I need you to listen to Kingston. Be as quiet as you can. If they hear you, they'll come."

I bob my head, blinking the tears from my eyes.

"Take her to the bathroom and lock the door," Austin tells Kingston. He turns to Diego. "Back me up?"

Diego gives me a once-over and subtly nods. "We'll be quick, beautiful. And we promise we'll do the best we can."

Kingston carries me to the bathroom, and we watch his brothers disappear out the front door. Pausing, Kingston listens for a second at the closed door.

And then he swears.

Spinning around, he flies us toward Diego's room instead of into the night after his brothers. Without him having to say, I know something's wrong. Someone's inside the cabin with us. I can hear the footsteps on the tile.

Kingston sets me on my feet in front of the weapons displayed on the wall. He picks out a small dagger and a scary ass sword. Without a word, he holds the dagger to me. The cool metal freezes my fingers, and I adjust it in my hand and hold it the way Diego taught me to give me the greatest distance if I have to use it.

With his hand, Kingston nudges me behind him, sandwiching me against the wall. He won't actively seek the intruder out and risk exposing me to danger, but waiting here, listening to the thuds of footsteps, ignites fear inside me.

Another set of footsteps sounds out, and my heart picks up pace. Kingston holds his finger to his lips, motioning for me to stay quiet. If only I could do something about my heart. About my labored breathing.

"Over here," a deep, raspy voice says through the crack in the door.

Kingston growls, the scary ass sound reverberating through my bones. "I'm giving you one opportunity to leave the premises," he says, his voice remaining even.

"You're outnumbered," a man says. "Hand over the donor, and we'll go."

"Fuck that," Kingston says. "She's mine."

I don't get the chance to brace myself before the door to the room flies off the hinges. Three vampires enter the room at a speed I nearly miss. If they weren't headed straight for us, I wouldn't be able to see them clearly at all.

Another loud ass roar echoes through the room, and I release a relieved breath at the towering form of Diego rushing into the room. He intercepts the vampires, knocking one of them into the wall.

I expect them to continue to attempt to come at me, but they race back and surround Diego, focusing on trying to take him down first.

"Kingston," I say, my soft voice barely managing to sound out over the growls. "Help him."

"I got it, beautiful," Diego says.

The one second he took his focus off the vampires was all they needed. Diego flies off his feet and collides into the wall, leaving a huge ass crater. He drops to the floor on his hands and knees but doesn't get the chance to get up. The vampires go after him again, their silver eyes glowing brightly in the dark room with only light filtering in from the living room.

Diego gets to his feet as quickly as he fell and grabs ahold of the nearest guy's head. I watch Diego jerk a blade through the vampire's neck, and Kingston covers my eyes a little too late, not doing a good job, because I still see every-thing. Diego drops the vampire's head on top of his twitch-ing body.

And then one of the other assholes flashes his fangs and jumps on Diego, sinking his teeth into Diego's arm, surpris-ing him.

"No!" I screech. "Stop!"

"Kingston, get her out of—"

Diego yells and swings his arm, punching another vam-pire man in the throat so hard that he tumbles across the room in our direction. He catapults to his feet and crashes into Kingston, squishing me into the wall. I gasp and sputter as the air knocks from my lungs. Kingston's weight falls off of me, and I collapse to the floor, hitting my knees hard enough to make me cry.

Fear explodes through me, and I scramble to my feet but don't make it far before Kingston and the vampire roll together toward me and send me spilling to the floor. Two strong hands wrap around my waist, picking me up. I screech and twist, catching sight of Gerald as he drags me out of the way.

"I got ya, Ms. Divine," he says, shielding me in the cor-ner of the room with his body. "You're gonna be all right. Your misters are fierce fighters. I've seen them take down a dozen vampires before."

I clutch onto his shoulders, peeking at the blurring forms crashing around the room. "You're okay," I whisper.

"I wouldn't have been without you. Mr. Divine got to me in time, and I know it was you who asked him to do so. Which I'm grateful for."

He yanks the collar of his shirt down to reveal two still-bleeding puncture wounds. I suck in a sharp breath and put pressure on his wound for him, using the collar of his shirt. He tenses every time a figure blurs near us, but he never makes a sound. He doesn't try to shove me away from him either. He stands tall, protecting me, and I can't help thinking about my dad. He'd do something like this. He'd never run or put his life over another.

A vampire smashes into the wall next to us, and I scream and jerk the knife I'm gripping for dear life at him. It sinks deep into the vampire's chest, and he convulses and throws himself back, taking the knife with him.

Austin's quick to grab him and shoves him into the wall, holding him in place. They snarl at each other, flashing their fangs, sending all sorts of panic through me.

"It wouldn't be so bad if these shadow vamps weren't so damn starved," Gerald mutters. "Hunger will drive anyone mad."

His words never rang truer. I should know. I've spent most of my life hungry.

"Why don't they just feed them?" I ask him.

"This is neutral territory. No one on the board wants to take responsibility. These assholes got kicked out of their regions for something or another."

"You know a lot about vampire politics."

Gerald doesn't get the chance to respond. A shadow vampire crashes through the nearby window and jumps right on him. I fall back and hit my head on the wall. Stars burst in my vision, and I blink a few times through the haze. A freaky, snow-covered man flashes his fangs at Gerald and exposes his neck.

"No!" I scream from my spot on the floor. "Don't! You don't want him."

The vampire snarls at me and bites into Gerald's throat despite my pleas. Gerald's mouth opens in a silent scream, and I search my surroundings. I find a knife on the floor only a few feet away, discarded from the weaponry wall. Scooping it up, I rush the few feet to the shadow vamp and Gerald.

"Damn it, babe!" Kingston yells. "Don't you dare try to fig—"

I surprise the hell out of every vampire in the room by slicing the knife across the palm of my hand. It's a distraction enough that the shadow vampire releases Gerald, dropping him to the floor. He doesn't make it even a foot toward me. Kingston comes up behind him and slings his arm over the vampire's neck. Austin steps between us, releasing the most unsettling, deep noise from his throat. Diego hooks his fingers around my waist, pulling me close.

"You're in so much trouble, babe." Kingston flares his nostrils. "Naughty list for eternity. And not the good kind."

"But Gerald, he—"

"You're going to bring any nearby intruders right to us," Kingston says, interrupting me. "Not to mention you're wasting all that fucking delicious blood."

Blood. Of course. My mom used to tell me that I'm more than what my vein can offer, but in this moment, my vein can offer a lot. It'll chill everyone out. Maybe even stop the fighting.

"Then give me a cup," I say, turning to Diego.

He raises his brows at me. "Please don't tell me you're considering doing what I think you're doing, beautiful."

I suck my bottom lip between my teeth. "They're hungry."

"So am I," Kingston quips. "But you don't see me acting like a raging lunatic."

I narrow my eyes at him. "Dude."

"No, Jewel," he says. "Don't *dude* me. It's not going to work. You're our girl, and there's no damn way I'm allowing you to offer your blood to—"

"What about the gen. pop. blood you have stashed away?" I keep my face expressionless to his comment. Because really, I most definitely agree with him. The thought of me feeding anyone other than my guys makes me uncomfortable.

"That's backup," he says.

"Oh, come on, Kingston," Diego says. "You don't even drink the fucking stuff anymore."

"And can't you tell Jewel's trying to help?" Austin adds.

"But—"

"Please, Kingston. I can't stand the fighting. I'm scared." Straightening my shoulders, I step an inch forward, pushing Austin to move so that I can close the space a bit. "It's the holidays. What if you were that guy?"

"Are you seriously asking me to envision myself as...him?" he mutters, shifting the vampire in his arms.

It's then that I realize he's stopped fighting. His silver eyes lock onto my every movement, staring at my bloody hand.

"Yes."

"I don't want to."

Diego sighs and disappears from my side only to return with a duffle bag. "Because you know it sucks."

Kingston fake-glares at me and sighs. "Sucking's fun, but oh-fucking-kay. I'm only agreeing for our girl." He shakes the vampire a few times. "You got that?"

Austin takes my hand in his. "And we expect you to leave and take your coven with you. If you don't, we'll consider it an act of war. This area will be swept clean, if you know what I mean."

"I'll see to it myself," Diego says.

The vampire flares his nostrils, glancing to me once more. I stiffen under his gaze and hold my breath because he's not quick to agree. But then he nods his head. Kingston loosens his grip but doesn't let him go. The vampire snatches the duffle bag and flashes his fangs at me in what I think might be a smile. *Happy friggin' holiday to you too, man.*

Kingston and Diego both chase him out of the cabin and disappear. I turn and spot Gerald on the floor, clutching his neck. Austin beats me to him and kneels down to inspect the deep bite mark. I crouch, balancing on the balls of my feet by supporting myself on Austin's shoulders.

"Can you help him, Austin?" I ask, trying to get a better look at the bite as Austin eases Gerald's hands from it.

Austin presses his hand down on the wound. "I need my kit."

I hop up and run to get it, but Diego materializes in the doorway to the room and brings the medical bag to Austin. We watch in silence as Austin tends to Gerald's wounds.

"He's going to be in pain for a bit but will survive. No

arteries were damaged." Austin swivels and takes my hurt hand to inspect it. "He was lucky that you're the bravest human I know."

"Our fierce girl," Diego says.

Kingston's groan sounds out from the living room. "I can't believe you did that."

"I can," Diego says, chuckling.

"You're still in trouble, babe," Kingston quips.

I smirk. "Good trouble, I hope. I hear the naughty list is fun."

A warm hand touches the top of mine, drawing my attention away from the silver flashing in Kingston's eyes. Gerald shifts up on an elbow and squeezes my good hand in his. He offers me a weak smile, and I return one to him, so glad to see his eyes focusing on me.

"You're going to be fine in no time," I tell him. "And thank you. For protecting me."

"It was nothing, Ms. Divine. I always knew the others were wrong about you," he whispers. "You're not a traitor to humanity. You're a gift."

I blink at his words. The only people to ever call me a traitor to humanity were Blood Rebels.

"My holiday miracle," he adds before closing his eyes.

Kingston, Diego, and Austin all look at Gerald and then to each other. They share a long, silent look, but soft footsteps from the living room steal their attention. Mitchell and the silver-haired vampire stand in the doorway with indecipherable expressions.

"You found my donor," the silver-haired vampire says. "What a treat."

Diego scoops Gerald into his arms and carries him across the room. "He saved my Blood Match and will be heavily rewarded."

I get to my feet and take a few small steps toward them, but Austin and Kingston each take one of my hands, stopping me.

"We expect you to take good care of this particular donor. He'll serve a great purpose on your staff," Kingston says.

"Of course, Mr. Divines. A donor loyal enough to protect a future Divine Heir will have a good life." The vampire turns his gaze to me, but he doesn't say anything.

He takes Gerald from Diego and vanishes, leaving me in a mess of emotions because I'm nearly certain I'll never see the man who always picked me flowers again. Mitchell searches the room, trailing his eyes over every broken piece of furniture, blood spot and body part, and damaged wall. He doesn't frown though. He surprises me by smiling at his sons.

"Looks like you all had a rather eventful time, my sons. I know how a good fight over the holidays brings you great pleasure." He swings his attention to me. "I do hope you appreciate the great lengths my heirs go through to protect you. I imagine our futures together will be ones of immeasurable power."

"Entertaining is one way to put it," Kingston says, side-glancing me in his peripheral vision. "But I think it's time we go."

Mitchell's jaw tightens. "So soon?"

Austin, Diego, and Kingston look at each other, and then Austin responds, "Jewel's been injured, and I feel it best that we take her home to heal. I hope you don't mind."

"I'll be sure to stop by on my way back to Dark Terrace Ranch," he says. "And if you don't mind, I'll be taking our new donor with me."

My guys all respond with a nod before I have a chance to ask him which donor from the group he got. Not that it matters. Stupid curiosity.

"Enjoy the rest of the holiday, my sons." Mitchell crosses the room and proffers his hand to me. I let him take mine in his, and he kisses the back of my knuckles. "Jewel, I do hope you had a lovely time despite the interruptions."

"I did, thanks," I say.

Surprisingly, it's true. The holiday might not have gone as my guys planned, but it was perfect despite that. We managed to save a life that would've been lost and hopefully satiated a few desperate vampires at least for a few days.

Mitchell squeezes each of my guys' shoulders and disappears from sight, leaving a flurry of snow swirling in through the door in his wake.

"You are way too nice, babe. The holiday sucked and not in a good way," Kingston says, smirking at me.

I turn to him and cup his cheeks. "Not all of it. And there's still time for—"

"Your next words better imply the good kind of sucking because it's all I want right now." He scoops me up and spins me off my feet.

I laugh. "Are you starved?"

"Like an angry shadow vampire."

Diego pulls me from Kingston and into a hug when he sets me down. "Careful, bro. She looks a little starved herself."

"Which I'll fix on the way home," Austin says, hugging me next.

I grin and kiss him. "Sounds like a plan to me."

Diego steps even closer, crowding me with Austin in the best way possible. "Then we'll watch all the old holiday classics in bed and watch the sunrise."

"And you can't forget the gifts," Kingston says, hooking his arms around all of us. "Or the blood."

I giggle and gently graze my teeth over his shoulder.

"Always with the blood, dude."

"Well, you did wish that we had the bloodiest holiday."

"And one with cuddles," I say, grinning.

Austin kisses my cheek. "We can definitely manage that."

BEST HOLIDAY EVER

COOL LIPS BRUSH OVER MY shoulder, and I turn over and into Diego's arms. The lowering sun glows through the tinted glass window, setting the sky ablaze in vivid pinks. Pulling the blanket up, I cover our heads and lean in to kiss Diego.

"Just a few minutes longer," I whisper, burying my face into his taut chest.

"Whatever you want, beautiful. What time did you fall asleep anyway?" he asks, tilting my chin up to kiss me. "I didn't mean to pass out before you."

I roll on top of him and return his kiss with one of my

own that tightens his hold around my waist. "You needed sleep. I needed to watch the next two movies on the playlist."

"Two?" Diego asks, combing his fingers through my hair to push it behind my ears instead of letting it veil around our faces.

I shift my legs to straddle him. "I think I'm addicted. I had no idea there were so many. I only had one in my collection, and it was nothing like these."

He chuckles, moving his lips from mine to kiss my jaw. "You can watch them all you want. I don't mind."

"Second chances are the best. So are fake relationships turned real. Secret princes. Miracles. Holiday switches."

"Did you see the one about a giant elf?"

I pull back slightly to see if he's joking, but with one look into his beautiful eyes, I know he's not. And now I want to watch it. "No, but I'm about to."

Diego laughs and snuggles against me, not letting me pull the blankets from our heads. "Just a few more minutes," he says, using my words against me. "I want this moment with you more than anything."

"More than anything?" I ask.

"Mmmhmm." His voice hums over my skin, sending tingles through me.

"How could I resist?" I tease, sliding my hands around his neck. "It is the last day of the Days of The Divide after all."

"And the first official day of Winter Nights."

"Which means more time with you doing whatever we want," I say playfully.

"Whatever?" he asks.

I answer him with a kiss so passionate that it leaves him moaning deep in his throat. There's nothing more I want from this moment than to shower Diego with my affection after everything that happened on Mount Crescent.

Rolling onto me, Diego awakens my body with the weight of his, and I kiss him harder at the feeling of his excitement pressing into me through my underwear. His fingers comb along the messy tresses of my hair, pushing it from my throat. His mouth wanders to my jaw to trail down my neck. I dig my fingers into Diego's shoulders, just enjoying his kisses and touch.

His fangs click the longer he gently sucks my throat, and I want nothing more than to give him what he desires. But he doesn't ask to bite me. All he does is continue to kiss me and explore my skin with his fingers, sliding them lower to make me gasp.

"I love you, beautiful," Diego whispers, gently exploring me as I open my legs a little more. "You have no idea how happy I am to wake up to you next to me."

I shift under him, braving to touch the skin just above

his waistband. "I think I do know."

"If only my brothers weren't about to knock on the door."

With his words, a tap sounds on the door, and I grin and cop a feel of exactly what me waking up next to Diego does to him. He releases another moan and buries his face into my neck, inhaling a deep breath of my skin a moment before kissing it.

"This is what I get for always joking with Kingston that the universe is against him," he murmurs at the sound of another knock.

"There's only one thing against you right now," I tease.

He presses harder to me and groans, but instead of giving into my affection, he eases up and puts an inch of space between us. "Shit, Kingston's going to bust down the door."

"You can hear him?" I ask.

"And we can hear you too, babe," Kingston calls out. "You do realize you suck at whispering when you're tired or excited. Definitely horny. So, please, pull that sexy ass together and stop making us jealous. Time to invite us in. And Diego, you promised that we could do this now. It's tradition."

Diego groans and flips off me only to take me with him. "Happy fucking Winter Nights, brothers," Diego says. "I hope you remember this next year if it falls on your night.

Go ahead and come in."

The door to the room flies open, and Kingston comes rushing in, his arms full of so many sparkling bags and boxes that my mouth falls agape at the sight. Austin strolls in after him, carrying a big ass tree full of ornaments and twinkling lights.

"Whoa, what is all of this?" I ask, climbing off Diego's lap to watch Kingston and Austin blur as they set up the Christmas tree and pile of presents that looks just like the ones from all the movies I stayed up late watching.

"Our gift exchange," Kingston says. "Something for everyone. But you first. I can't wait any longer."

I turn to Diego, who gets to his feet, and he motions for me to cross the room because he knows I want to. Austin meets me half way, beating Kingston, and pulls me into a hug. He kisses me sweetly on the lips and steps back, trailing his gaze from my head to my feet.

"How are you feeling?" he asks, taking a quick look at my nearly healed hand.

"Amazing," I respond, swinging his hand once. "And happy Winter Nights, Austin. This looks incredible."

"So do you, babe," Kingston says. "Now come here so I can take a moment to enjoy that nightie. I thought for sure I'd be stumbling into a view of never-ending flannel."

I laugh and skip closer, throwing my arms around him.

"Yeah, sure, Kingston. All the long stuff went missing."

He raises his eyebrow. "Wasn't me."

Diego chuckles and slides his hands around my waist. "Sorry, beautiful. I just wanted to be the thing to keep you warm."

My cheeks burn with blush, and I whip my head, sending my hair splaying back and forth. Diego guides me forward, and we take a seat on the plush carpet between his brothers. Austin pops the lid off a white box, and I practically drool all over the place at the sight of all the colorful doughnuts.

"This is too much." I let Austin hold up a doughnut with red and green sprinkles to my mouth.

"Never," Kingston says. "We promised a perfect holiday, and we never break our promises. Now, here. Open my gift to you first. It's the best one."

I smirk and take the thin, square-shaped package into my hands. A silver bow shines with my reflection, and I just take a minute to look at the pretty packaging.

"It's okay to tear into it, babe." Kingston nudges my knee with his knuckles. "That's the point."

I stick my tongue out at him and playfully stretch my leg out to kick him. "Give me a minute to enjoy it."

"I'll give you all the minutes, hours, days—actually, you'll have an entire year to enjoy it. But you have to open it first."

My brows pucker at his comment, and I slide my finger into the sparkly paper and tear it, ripping it free. I stare in surprise at the first paper calendar I've ever seen in my life. My whole body buzzes as I trail my eyes over a provocative photo of Kingston in his boxer briefs on the cover. The image makes me blush so friggin' hard I cover it with my hand.

"Damn," I whisper.

Austin and Diego groan in unison. "Really, Kingston?" Diego asks.

"Fuck yeah. Can't you see how much our girl loves it? One hundred, sexy ass percent for body match. Go on, babe. Flip it open."

I turn my gaze to Kingston, my heart ramming against my ribcage. "Later."

"Just the first page."

"Fuck," I whisper under my breath.

He snickers and nudges my knee with his hand again. When I'm not quick to move, he scoots closer and flips the first page for me, and I cover my face with my hand. "This is the most interesting gift I've ever gotten."

"Hot, right?"

I lean into him and press my lips to his ear. "I don't think my body will ever recover."

He moans and trails his fingers higher up my leg. "Glad

you like it."

Turning slightly, I kiss him. "Love it."

Diego and Austin both look at each other, shaking their heads, and I inhale another small breath and fan myself. Kingston grins and shifts away from me, reaching for the pile of presents again. "These two are from those guys. Try to hide the fact that you're unimpressed. I guess I should've given you the best ever present last."

I playfully smack my hand to his shoulder and put Kingston's calendar face down on the carpet. Diego scoots closer and picks up the dark blue, glittery package Kingston set in front of me and hands it over. "I know this isn't as creative, or as *interesting* as Kingston's, but I think you'll like it."

Tearing open the paper, I pop the lid off the box. Inside, I find what looks like an oversized tablet. Diego takes it from my hands and clicks a button on the back. The screen lights up with a picture of the four of us that Walt, the head of security took for us in the garden in front of the pond. The screen flashes, and a video of me and Kingston laughing and dancing in the middle of his room pops up next. The four of us watch the slideshow of a mixture of pictures of the four of us from the last few weeks.

And then a picture of my cousins and Ramona pops up on screen.

Tears trickle from my eyes, and I hold the picture box to my chest for a moment.

"Really, Diego? You made our girl cry on—"

I sniffle and smile. "Happy tears. I love it."

Diego engulfs me into a hug, and then Austin and Kingston both join us, squeezing me between them. "Happy Winter Nights, Diego," I murmur. "And thanks."

Diego kisses me. "Glad you like it."

Austin holds his hands out for me, and I peel myself away from Diego and settle into Austin's lap. He picks up the metallic red box from the floor and sets it on my lap, resting his chin on my shoulder.

I pull out a small leather journal with an imprint of my vow pendant stained on the front. I run my fingers over it and smile. "It's beautiful, Austin."

"Open it," he says, kissing my shoulder.

I flip the book open and read the inscription.

Jewel, here is to an unforgettable forever full of love, hope, and adventure.

Eternally yours,
Austin

A smile crosses my face, and I turn the page over. A picture of me and Austin is attached to it with the vow Austin promised me the night he asked me to transform into a vampire and to be a true Divine written under it.

"Diego's and Kingston's are in there too," he says, reaching out to flip the pages to show me. "And the rest is for you to fill in. So you always remember life over our forever."

I swivel in his arms and attack him with my lips, kissing him a dozen times. I motion for Kingston to come to me next so that I can give him just as much affection. Diego laughs when Kingston scoops me up and tosses me to him, and he meets me for a kiss as sweet as his blood. This moment couldn't have been any more perfect, and sitting here with the three guys I'm madly in love with is the best gift I could have ever gotten.

"Now, it's time for your gifts," I say, pushing to my feet. "From me."

"Our gifts?" Kingston asks.

I beam him a smile and nod. "Diego couldn't handle an entire day of Christmas movies, so I took advantage of my time alone."

"You fell asleep on our girl?" Kingston asks.

Diego throws an empty box at Kingston and misses him. "You just wait for your night. I created a twenty hour collection."

Kingston glares. "No TV in bed in our room. It's only

for sex and sleeping."

It's my turn to throw an empty box at him. He laughs, letting it hit him in the head. "We'll see about that, dude."

He snaps his teeth at me, beaming a smile.

I turn my back on the three of them, feeling the heat of their gazes drinking me in. I purposely sway my hips a little more than usual, sending the short nightie back and forth in a teasing view that has them holding their breaths.

Strolling to the nightstand, I open the top drawer and pull out the three envelopes with the gifts I spent hours during my Christmas movie marathon making. I know they told me that having me around is a gift in itself, but I still wanted to do something. And I'm glad I did.

"First, I have to say, gift giving to the vampires that have everything was hard," I say. "And I know this might be cheesy, and they're not as good as what you've given me...but here."

I hand each of them the envelopes with their names on it and hug myself, shifting on my feet as I watch them open it.

"Fuck yeah, babe!" Kingston says, hopping to his feet. He tackles me, knocking me off mine but turns in the air so that I land on top of him on the floor. "These are damn perfect, and I'm turning them all in now."

I laugh breathlessly and push up on his chest. "You have

to wait for your night."

He fake glares at me. "There was no fine print."

"Check again, Kingston," Austin says. "It's right here on the back."

Kingston groans. "Damn it. You've read too many contracts. I really wanted you to—" Flipping through the handmade book with activities I wrote specifically for him on each page, he stops on the second to last one. "Feed me in bed. Right now. I'm starved."

"You're always starved," I murmur.

"That makes two of us," Diego says.

"Three," Austin adds.

I laugh and smile at them. "I think I could do something about that."

"You first, Jewel," Austin says. "We can wait."

"And so can I. This is your holiday," I say. "You've done enough for me. Let me do this for you."

"Just what I wanted, beautiful," Diego says.

Austin grins and knocks his fist to his brother's. "I have to agree with that. I'll get my kit."

I step closer, swallowing my nerves. "Actually, since it *is* a special occasion, I was thinking you could just...bite me."

Kingston flashes his fangs. "Best holiday ever."

~The End~

Thank you so much for reading *Blood Holiday*! I hope you enjoyed this festive story! Find out what Jewel and the Divines are up to in *Blood Debt*, the third installment of *The Divine Vampire Heirs* series.

To stay up-to-date on new and future releases, make sure to sign up for Ginna's newsletter or join her Facebook Group Paranormal Center for Matches and Mates. You'll also get exclusive access to special content, including *Divine Blood*, a serialized re-telling of *Blood Match* from your favorite blood brothers' points of view.

ACKNOWLEDGMENTS

THANKS SO MUCH TO KATIE for her hard work and her enthusiasm during the creation of this story. Without her pressure and excitement for a bloody Christmas, *Blood Holiday* might not have existed. Your love of holiday stories is finally wearing off on me, Katie. Bah humbug.

Another special thanks goes to the ladies of Write Bitches. Your support and encouragement means the world to me.

Lastly, thanks to you, dear reader. Your love of the Divines means the world to me. XOXO!

ABOUT GINNA MORAN

GINNA MORAN IS a writer from sunny Southern California. She started writing poetry as a teenager in a spiral notebook that she still has tucked away on her desk today. Her love of writing grew after she graduated high school, and she completed her first unpublished manuscript at age eighteen.

When she realized her love of writing was her life's passion, she studied literature at Mira Costa College in Northern San Diego. Besides writing novels, she was senior editor, content manager, and image coordinator for Crescent House Publishing Inc. for four years.

Aside from Ginna's professional life, she enjoys binge

watching television shows, playing pretend with her daughter, and cuddling with her dogs. Some of her favorite things include chocolate, anything that glitters, cheesy jokes, and organizing her bookshelf.

Ginna Moran loves to hear from her readers so visit her online at www.GinnaMoran.com. You can also find her on Facebook, Twitter, and Instagram. To stay up-to-date on new releases, sign up to her newsletter. You'll not only get exclusive access to extra stories, but you'll be able to participate in monthly giveaways!

www.ingramcontent.com/pod-product-compliance
Lightning Source LLC
Chambersburg PA
CBHW062023190726
48284CB00014B/2638